JAN 2 4 2008 DATE DUE			
NelCat	2-5-18		

14

Long Journey Home

JULIUS LESTER

LONG JOURNEY HOME

Stories from Black History

J FICTION

DIAL BOOKS   NEW YORK

Published by Dial Books
A Division of Penguin Books USA Inc.
375 Hudson Street
New York, New York 10014

Text copyright © 1972 by Julius Lester
Jacket painting copyright © 1972 by Charles Lilly
All rights reserved
Printed in the U.S.A.
Reissue, 1993
1 3 5 7 9 10 8 6 4 2
Typography by Atha Tehon

Library of Congress Cataloging in Publication Data
Lester, Julius.
  Long journey home.
  Contents: Satan on my track.—Louis.—Ben. [etc.]
  [1. African Americans—Fiction] I. Title.
PZ7.L5629Lo3   [Fic.]   75-181791

For
Those who went before
and
Alice Walker
who knows

Foreword

These stories are based on historical fact. (See Notes p. 149.) That is, they actually happened and there is documentation to substantiate them. I have taken liberties and added details of character and setting consistent with the period, as well as creating additional characters in some instances and character motivation where it was lacking in the original source material. Any writer of historical fiction does the same as a means of intensifying the human experience in the story, and as a means of teaching history.

For me these stories, and hundreds like them, comprise the essence of black history. They are not the stories of the lives and works of so-called great men and women who generally make up history as we know it. While it is necessary to know of Harriet Tubman, Frederick Douglass, Sojourner Truth, and many other figures in black history, they comprise only one facet of that history. They are thought of as leaders and others as followers. I prefer to think of the "great figures" as individuals who embodied in their lives and actions the ethos of their times, and for that reason stand out above the mass. The mass, however, were the movers of history. While Frederick Douglass organized against slavery, he would have been an isolated figure if hundreds of thousands of slaves had not run away, eventually threatening slavery's survival to such an extent that the South was forced to go to war. History is made by the many, whose individual deeds are seldom recorded and who are never known outside their own small circles of friends and acquaintances. It is merely represented by the "great figures," who are symbols, reflectors of the history being made by the mass.

J.L.

Contents

SATAN ON MY TRACK

On Saturday afternoon there was scarcely anyone on the Bryant plantation. Monday to Friday they worked in the fields from the time the sun was a half-circle of orange over the eastern edge of the world until it was a half-circle of red over the western edge. On Saturday, though, they were allowed to stop working while the sun still glared from the top of the sky. They laid their hoes across their shoulders and with much laughing and talking went to their shacks, washed, put on clean clothes, and started

2

for Bryantown, a mile and a half of dusty road to the south. Many walked, but those who could squeezed onto already crowded mule wagons. By the time the wagons got to town, sometimes there were people hanging from the sides, their feet dragging in the dust. It was Saturday, and only those too old or too sick stayed behind.

Bryantown was two small frame houses across from the railroad tracks at the southern end of the plantation. The train went by twice a day, but no one had ever known it to stop. Who would be getting off at Bryantown? And no one would be leaving. Not without Cap'n Bryant's permission, and no one dared ask for such. Cap'n Bryant had been known to kill niggers for less.

Although everyone called it Bryantown, it didn't appear on any maps or government records. It wasn't really a town, and even if it had been, that word would not have been an adequate or accurate description. In reality it was a small country of some four hundred acres of rich Mississippi delta land, five hundred blacks, including children and infants, ruled by Cap'n Bryant. He owned the land and the shacks the people lived in, sold them the food they ate, the clothes they wore on their backs, the cottonseed they put in the ground, and the tools they farmed with. And although slavery had been declared illegal sixty years before, the blacks within Cap'n Bryant's four hundred acres lived no differently than their parents and grandparents had, some of whom still lived and remembered the

3

day Cap'n Bryant's father had told them they were free.

On Saturday afternoon Cap'n Bryant could be found in the second of the two frame shacks. This was the store, or commissary, as it was called. It was well stocked with chewing tobacco, snuff, brightly colored bolts of cloth for dresses and shirts, fatback and grits, patent medicines, and, of course, moonshine whiskey. All afternoon Cap'n Bryant stood behind the counter, taking items from the shelves and noting the price beside the person's name in his ledger book. Back during slavery his father had decided what the niggers needed and passed it out to them. Cap'n Bryant believed in treating his niggers a little better. He let them come to the commissary and get whatever they wanted.

On Saturday people went to the commissary first to do their buying and pay their respects to "de ducks." They stood at the counter and watched while Cap'n Bryant added another figure to the long line of figures already under their names and wondered if at settlin' up time "de ducks" were going to keep them in debt for another year.

"Well, de ducks got me again this year," one would say jokingly to another on that cold November day when they lined up outside the commissary to settle their accounts. "Cap'n Bryant look in that big book of his and he say he deduck for the medicine I had to have for my chillun, and he deduck for the cottonseed and the new plow and the new shoes and clothes and the chewing tobacco and the snuff for my mama and the moonshine and the food and the rent. And he put all de ducks together and he say, 'Well, Sam, you owed me two hundred dollars from last year and the cotton you and your family raised this year brought in nine hundred dollars. You did real good this year, Sam. But y'all spent 'leven hundred dollars for rent and the cottonseed and that new plow and all the rest. So that mean you end up owing me four hundred dollars. Sho' am sorry about that, Sam. Thought you was gon' get out of debt this year. Well, you work hard like a good boy and I believe you might make it out of debt next settlin'-up time.' " Sam, or whoever it was, since all their stories were the same, would shake his head. "It's like my ol' poppa used to say. An ought's an ought. A figger is a figger. All for the white man. None for the nigger." Everyone would laugh, hearing the words of the old ones again. And their laughter was the laughter of the old ones.

After paying their respects to "de ducks" they moved outside to drink their moonshine, play cards, shoot dice, and do whatever else might be necessary to forget the week that had passed and to push away the week that was coming. By nightfall, though, most had started back to their shacks to go to bed and rise early for church the next morning. Some remained, however, and moved inside the other building of Bryantown, the café. No one knew why it was called that since no food was served. It was merely a big room with chairs and tables where the serious Saturday night gambling and drinking took place. Generally a guitar player was there, too, playing and singing the blues that inhabited the lives of the listeners like another heart.

In the far corner of the café, near the door, sat a big dark-skinned man with a .45 in a holster strapped around his waist. Black Emmett they called him behind his back. He was in charge of the café and was Cap'n Bryant's right-hand man. They also called him Cap'n Bryant's nigger, because instead of working in the fields it was his job to keep order among the blacks. Emmett was hated, but he didn't care. At least he didn't have to get out in the fields and work like a mule. Cracking a drunk nigger's head was easier and more fun than picking cotton. And he didn't have to stand in line at settlin'-up time. He got paid in cash.

Emmett could see the entire room from the corner. The figures were mere silhouettes in the faint light of the coal-oil lamps on each table, but Emmett didn't watch people. He looked for motion, any kind of unusual motion which would indicate that somebody was reaching for a knife or gun or that a fight was starting. He didn't understand why Cap'n Bryant cared if the niggers killed each other. Who would notice one nigger less? Understanding or not, he was supposed to stop them from killing one another. Most of the time he did. But sometimes the first thing he knew was that someone was screaming. Emmett would get a couple of men to drag the body outside and Saturday night would continue on its way toward Sunday morning.

It was late afternoon when Rambler came into town, his guitar across his back. He was a medium-sized dark-skinned man whose skin seemed to glow black from someplace deep inside. His black color swallowed his facial features and even the whites of his eyes seemed to be hiding in the surrounding darkness. His large lips were set in a straight line, and even when he smiled, showing his white teeth, his mouth didn't appear to like the smile. As he stood on the railroad tracks looking across the field at the commissary and café, his arms hung loosely at his sides. He held his head erect and his shoulders weren't stooped and bent from a life of cotton.

After many moments he walked slowly down the embankment toward the people clustered in small groups outside the café and commissary. He hadn't wanted to stop at the little town whose name he didn't know. It was too small. He wouldn't make more than two dollars and all the whiskey he could drink. But two dollars was more than he had, and it was late and he was tired. He had been walking the tracks all day.

"Looks like we got us a guitar player," said a voice as he walked up.

Someone else laughed. "Somebody better go tell Joe Jr. that he got some competition tonight."

Rambler heard them but gave no indication that he had. Joe Jr., he snorted to himself. On every plantation there was somebody who thought he could play the blues. Sometimes he could. But none of them could stand up to him. He was Rambler! He could make a guitar do everything except pick cotton and chew tobacco. He hoped Joe Jr. wouldn't get angry when the people started telling him to shut up so "this here new man can play." That was always the way it went. Sometimes he would find himself in a fight with the local blues picker who until that night had been king of the roost. Rambler had to be careful of the women, too. He'd never understood why, but it seemed like women just couldn't resist a guitar player. Many nights he had come close to getting killed by some plantation hand who thought Rambler was trying to take his woman.

"Can you play that box?" someone asked.

He nodded. "I reckon I can," he responded quietly.

"Well, let's go in the café here and just see."

"Yeah. Let's do that," someone else added. "Frankly, I don't think he know a thing 'bout no music."

"What yo' name, honey?" a woman came up to him and asked.

"Rambler."

"Rambler what?"

"Just Rambler."

"Where you from?" someone else wanted to know.

He shrugged. "I don't know."

"You don't know? Aw, man, what kinna story is that?"

"You ain't running from the law, is you?" someone else asked.

"Uh-uh," Rambler replied.

"Then how come you don't want to say where you from?"

" 'Cause I don't know." He was telling the truth. The last time he'd seen his mother had been six years ago. He'd been fifteen then. One night, when she and his brothers and sisters were asleep, he'd slung his guitar over his back when he'd heard the train whistle blow, run through the fields, and caught the freight as it slowed to enter the steep curve just before it crossed the river. That had been on the Fields plantation, outside Eland, Mississippi. But that wasn't where he was from. He didn't have a home and had nothing but contempt for anyone who called a shack on a white man's plantation a home. Not him. Even when he was a little boy being taught to pick cotton by his mother, he knew he was going to get out of those fields as soon as he could. Cotton! Everybody's life was ruled by it, from the spring rains when the plowing and planting began until late November when they went through the fields picking up the cotton scraps. And then, at settlin'-up time, nothing. The cap'n would tell you that maybe next year you could get out of debt if you worked a little harder. Uh-uh, Rambler said to himself. As long as the cap'n added up the figures there was no way anyone was going to get out of debt. That was why he had become a blues singer. He got up when he wanted to, went where he wanted to, and nobody could make him do otherwise. And he kept moving to make sure Satan never caught up with him.

Rambler walked with the people into the already crowded café. Behind the noise he could hear the sound of a guitar and a voice. He looked toward the front of the room and saw a medium-sized man in coveralls sitting on a chair, playing and singing. That must be Joe Jr., he thought. Rambler was scarcely listening, though, because he knew that Joe Jr. was singing to no one but himself. People were playing cards, laughing, talking, and not dancing. People didn't sit still when Rambler played. They couldn't. His music made them dance, whether they wanted to or not. Many nights people danced so much that the floor started to cave in and he'd had to stop playing to keep the house from literally falling down.

"Before you can play," someone said to him, "we got to talk to Emmett."

Rambler didn't need to be told who Emmett was. His name was always different but his job was the same. He was the white man's head nigger and anything that went on had to have the white man's approval. Rambler looked around the room until he saw the large dark-skinned man sitting in the corner behind him. "Is that him?"

"That's him. You know him?"

"Uh-huh," Rambler breathed to himself, turning and walking over to Emmett.

Emmett had had his eyes on Rambler from the instant he walked in, but now, as Rambler approached, Emmett pretended to be looking at the cards in his hand.

"How much you pay for a guitar player?" Rambler asked.

Emmett didn't look up or give any indication that he'd heard. He'd seen Cap'n Bryant make a nigger wait five minutes before answering a question, and he had learned to make them wait, too. It was a way of letting them know who was boss when Cap'n Bryant wasn't around. After a couple of minutes he looked up, stared, and then laughed. "Damn! Here's a nigger blacker than me!" he shouted.

Everyone within hearing laughed.

"I'm gon' keep you 'round here," Emmett continued. "You make me look like I'm white."

Rambler's expression didn't change. "How much you pay?"

Emmett cut his laughter short. "We got a guitar picker. Or is you deaf? Anyway, Cap'n Bryant don't 'low no strange niggers on his place. Especially none blacker than me."

Rambler stared at Emmett for a moment, then turned and made his way to the other side of the room. He pulled his guitar around in front of him and, holding it close to his ear, tuned it. He pulled a cylindrical metal tube from his pocket and placed it on the little finger of his right hand. Then, without a word, he slid the piece of metal up the neck of the guitar as hard as he could. The sound of the metal against the steel guitar strings pierced through the noise of the crowd, and as he started playing, he heard a woman shout, "Play that thing, boy!"

"They call me Rambler," he sang loudly, " 'cause I'm rambling all the time." The guitar sang the last few notes back at him. "They call me Rambler," he repeated, " 'cause I'm rambling all the time." The guitar sang it back at him again. "I'd like to stay with you, baby, but I got to move on down the line." His eyes were closed, but he was singing directly to the woman who had shouted at him. "I got to ramble, 'cause Satan's on my track." His voice was rough and harsh from the countless Saturday nights he had had to make himself heard over the noise of crowds like this one. He seemed to growl rather than sing, but he'd never known anyone to complain. "I got to ramble, 'cause the Devil's on my track." As the guitar answered him, he knew that the people could almost see Satan walking down the road. "I got to keep goin', Lord, I can't look back."

"Sing your song, Guitar Man!" a voice shouted.

"Preach it!" came another.

A large woman in a cotton print dress got up and

started to dance, and Rambler knew that if Emmett tried to kick him out now, there would be a fight. He cut his eye toward Joe Jr., who was still sitting in the front of the room, smiling dumbly, his guitar lying across his lap. "I told my mama," he heard himself sing for the second time, "Mama, I'm leaving home."

"Sho' 'nuf!"

"The Devil will get me if I stay one place too long."

The sun had begun painting the gray clapboard front of the café orange by the time Rambler slung his guitar around to his back. The few people who were left begged him to play more, but he slid the metal tubing from his little finger, dropped it in his pocket, and walked over to the corner where Emmett sat.

"You pretty good, black boy," Emmett said without smiling.

"You ain't never heard better," Rambler said flatly.

Emmett nodded. "Might be. You got to be good to play on Cap'n Bryant's plantation without his say-so. Any other man done what you did without permission would've been carried out of here."

Rambler was tired and didn't feel like playing Emmett's little game. "Since Cap'n Bryant didn't have me thrown out, it must mean I was hired for the night."

"Cap'n Bryant pays his guitar pickers in whiskey."

"Well, I ain't one of *his*. I take mine in money."

Emmett was silent. He stared at Rambler and Rambler stared back. Neither smiled. Rambler knew that if he showed the slightest fear, he wouldn't get paid. But he wasn't afraid. There was a nigger like Emmett on every plantation. Big, mean, who did the cap'n's dirty work, no matter what it was. Niggers thought Emmett was tough, but Rambler knew better. Emmett was afraid of white people. Rambler wasn't.

Finally Emmett asked, "How much?"

"Five."

"You must be crazy, nigger!" Emmett shouted. "The most Cap'n Bryant ever paid was a dollar. You must be outta your mind."

"Cap'n Bryant never had a guitar picker like me on his place."

There was another long pause. Rambler knew he wouldn't get five dollars. But if he had said three, he would've ended up getting one.

"I'll give you three, and even at that Cap'n Bryant is going to cuss me out."

Rambler paused. "I'll take the three."

Emmett reached in his pocket and from a roll of bills pulled off three ones. "Here, nigger. How long you gon' be around?"

Rambler picked up the money from the table and put it in his pocket. "Leaving now."

"Folks liked your picking. I could talk to Cap'n Bryant. If I say so, he would let you stay and pay you three dollars a night every Friday and Saturday."

"I got to be moving."

Rambler walked outside into the early-morning sun. Already it was warm. He looked at the sky. It was clear and piercingly blue. It was going to be another hot day. A young girl stepped out from the side of the building and smiled at him.

"You not leaving already, Rambler?"

He looked at her. "I was thinking about it."

"Don't leave yet. Folks around here would like to get better acquainted with you." She walked up to him and took him by the arm and he allowed himself to be taken by her. He was tired, needed to sleep. So he went with her, as he had gone with someone the previous Saturday, the Saturday before that, and practically every Saturday in the past six years. There were some women who came to a guitar player as sure as a hunting dog came when you whistled.

The sun was going down when he woke up. He lay on the dirty mattress in a corner of the one-room shack and listened to the children playing outside. He assumed that they were the girl's. Lucille, he believed she'd said her name was. She didn't have a husband, but neither did some of the other women on the plantation. He wondered

if he had any children playing in the yard of some plantation as the sun was setting. Probably. The thought that
there might be a young Rambler somewhere didn't make
him happy. He knew it wasn't right, the way he came and
went. Yet what else was there? He either stayed on Cap'n
Bryant's plantation or Cap'n John's or Cap'n Wilson's
or Cap'n whoever's, or he rambled. And that was no
choice. Not for him.

He had known that on those evenings he had played
hide-and-go-seek as the children outside were doing now.
He had seen Cap'n Ross come to the cabin at night and
he knew what his mother did with him. And for a while,
when he'd been younger, he'd hated his mother for letting
that white man come to her bed. After Rambler left he
used to beat every woman he was with. He tried to love
them, but he only got mad and before he knew anything
he'd knocked the girl down, whoever she was. He didn't
do that now. He understood that his mother couldn't help
herself and that he had hated her because he was afraid
to hate the white man. Not any more he wasn't. All he had
to do was think of Cap'n Ross's rough hands pushing him
out of the bed he shared with his mother and making him
go outside. That was why he couldn't stay in one place.
Settle down and the white folks would start choking the
life out of you. Occasionally he met a girl whom he
would allow himself to dream about. He liked the pictures
he drew in his mind of them working hard together, rais-

16

ing children, buying some land, and building something. He liked that as well as the next man. But he didn't allow himself to really believe in the picture. Didn't matter whether his real name was Cap'n Bryant or Cap'n Ross, he was Satan. Never let a man have a minute's peace. Sometimes he thought white folks were put on earth just to make a nigger's life hard.

Not his, though. As long as he could pick a note on the guitar, white folks couldn't touch him. That was why they hated nigger music so much. It was free, and because it came from him, it meant he was free, too.

He turned over and looked at Lucille, who was sitting at the table in the middle of the room, lighting the coal-oil lamp. She was a pretty little girl, he thought. She was black like him. She wasn't the creation of some white man. Maybe one of these days he'd come back and get her, take her up North somewhere, where they would have some kind of chance. It was only a dream, though. He was married to the blues and had been since that night Charlie Burnett had come to see his mother and sat on the porch and played the blues. He couldn't have been more than six, but since that moment, his soul had belonged to the blues.

He began to hear music everywhere he went. It was in the air and all you had to do was listen. He could be in the field or walking down a road or playing in the yard and he'd hear the blues. He made his first guitar from a cigar box and copper wire when he was seven. It was almost impossible to play on it, but it was better than nothing. A few months later, though, his mother had bought him a guitar and from then on his mind was on music. He stopped playing with the other boys to spend all of his time with the blues pickers on the plantation. He must have worried them almost to death with his "Show me how you played that last song." But they would, and he'd go home and practice until it was time to go to bed, and then, after his mother was asleep, he'd go outside and sometimes play until the sun came up. At first his fingers weren't strong enough to push hard on the thin wire strings. You had to press the strings hard against the guitar neck, mash them flat, so that when you picked a string, it gave a loud, clear sound. The strings cut his fingertips, often making them bleed. Eventually, though, his fingertips became hardened and playing became easier. Many a morning he went to the fields without having slept. But he couldn't help himself. Once the blues got you, you had to give in to them.

He would never forget the night when he really became a blues singer. He had gone to bed with his mother as usual, but when she was asleep, he slipped outside. He walked a ways from the house so his playing wouldn't wake her. He had been playing different runs he knew on the instrument, not playing any song in particular, when he heard himself begin to sing: "Oh, look at the moon, shining down on me." He heard the guitar repeat the last notes of the line. "Oh, look at the moon, shining down on me," he sang again. The guitar repeated the last notes again. "Sitting here in this cottonfield down in Mississippi." He wondered where the words had come from. He hadn't thought of them. His mouth had simply opened and out had come the blues. "I'm sitting down here," the words came, "singing these old lonesome blues." The guitar said it in its way. "I'm sitting down here," he sang again, but this time the guitar completed the line by itself. "I ain't got nothing, not even a pair of shoes." Then he'd let the guitar talk for a while. It was as if his fingers had a life all their own, moving over the strings without him telling them what strings to pick. Then he heard himself singing, "I wonder sometimes if the moon ever gets the blues. Yes, I wonder sometimes if the moon ever gets the blues. I wonder sometimes if white folks ever lose."

After that the blues had never left him any peace. The words and the music were always there, ready to come out of him whenever he opened his mouth. He was only ten years old then, but he started playing for dances on the weekends. Cotton Sam would take him. He was the best blues picker around and was the closest thing to a father Rambler had ever had. By the time he was fourteen he was almost as good as Cotton Sam. The two of them played together every weekend, and Rambler saw everything there was to see, because at one time or another it happened at those Saturday night parties. Many was the night he and Sam had left a place through the window. When those niggers got drunk and the bullets got to flying around, nobody was safe.

One Saturday night Cotton Sam wanted him to go to a party, but for some reason he decided not to. It was the first time he hadn't gone with him. But that Saturday he hadn't particularly felt like playing. The next morning Cotton Sam was found dead on the railroad tracks. Some drunk white boys had seen him walking down the tracks toward his house and, for no reason, had beat him to death. Nobody thought too much about it. It happened all the time on plantations. White man got bored, had nothing to do, so he went out, got drunk, and killed a nigger. And since no white man was ever arrested for killing a nigger, Sam was buried as quietly as if he'd died of pneumonia.

He was given Sam's guitar after the funeral. He took it reluctantly, knowing that in some way he didn't understand he now became the keeper of Sam's soul. A man's guitar was more a part of him than a woman could ever be. And when he took the guitar in his hands, he knew that he was holding the real Sam. As long as he lived and played that guitar, Cotton Sam lived too.

The Saturday night after Sam was murdered, Rambler was supposed to play for a party, but with Cotton Sam's guitar on his back he hopped the freight. With Sam dead, there was no reason to stay. And he had been going ever since. It was Sam who'd given him the name Rambler, because he used to ask Sam to sing about "ramblin' " all the time.

He got out of bed and put on his clothes. "I got some chicken on the stove for you," Lucille said.

He smiled. "Thank you."

She took several pieces of chicken from the skillet, put them on a plate, and set it on the table. "Everybody wants to know where you gon' be playing at tonight. They want to get some whiskey and come over here and have a little party."

He shook his head. "Naw, I don't think so."

"How come?" she asked fearfully.

He bit into a piece of the chicken, but when he spoke he said, "You a good cook, Lucille. Real good."

She smiled shyly. "It ain't hard when you got somebody to cook for."

"Them your kids out in the yard?"

"Only one of 'em. His name is Paul."

"How old is he?"

"He be four in October."

Rambler finished the chicken rapidly. It'd been several days since he'd eaten that much. "You and the kid ate yet?"

"Uh-huh. You want some more?"

He nodded, knowing that she and the child hadn't eaten. She took his plate and put the rest of the chicken on it.

He looked at her, liking her more and more. "You live here by yourself? I mean, just you and the kid?"

"Uh-huh. My mama was living here, but she's laying over in the boneyard now. She died about a year ago and I been here by myself ever since."

"How come a girl pretty as you ain't got no man?"

She shrugged. "Who wants any of these no-count niggers? They don't know no more than I do. And all I know is cotton. I want somebody who knows something different than me. You never did answer my question. How come you ain't gon' play tonight? You don't feel like it?"

"That ain't it. I got to be moving along."

"Ain't you happy right now?"

He nodded. "I can tell you know how to make a man happy. But you know Cap'n Bryant ain't gon' have no nigger on his plantation who won't work in the field. And this is one that won't."

"Couldn't you just work in the field for a little while? Until I got out of debt and then we could go somewhere that the white folks wouldn't bother us?"

"Cap'n Bryant don't let niggers get out of debt."

He finished eating and got up slowly from the table. They stood looking at each other for a moment and he felt himself wanting to hug her tightly and say that everything would be all right, that he would always be there. But he couldn't. Even if he did stay, he knew that one morning the sun would come up and its light would glance off the railroad tracks and strike him in the eyes like a flash of lightning. There wouldn't be a thing he could do except sling his guitar on his back and go. So if you knew you were going, might as well do it sooner than later. It was easier for everybody that way. He walked over to the corner by the front door where he'd put his guitar, picked it up, and slung it on his back.

"Thanks for everything. If I ever come this way again, Lucille, I'll be sure and look you up." He paused, waiting for her to say something, but when she only looked at him, he turned and walked out the door.

The night was warm. A mosquito buzzed near his ear and flew away as he waved his hand at it. Far in the distance he heard the sound of a train whistle. *Whoo! Whoo!* He stopped in the yard to get his bearings. Six years of rambling had taught him to be observant, and when he had come that morning, he had seen the railroad a few hundred yards back of the house and the path going through the cottonfield toward it. He started toward the path when he heard footsteps behind him.

"There's a shortcut," she said, taking his hand in hers. "I'll be back in a minute, Paul!" she shouted into the darkness.

The whistle sounded again, this time a little closer.

"Every night when that train pass through here, I say to myself, One of these days, Lucille. I been hearing that train every night since I was born. And every time I hear it, you know, it reminds me of something, but I can't ever remember what. You know what I mean?"

"That's the way I feel, too. I didn't know nobody else ever felt that way. I thought it was just me."

"I ain't never heard nothing like it. So mournful. It makes me sad, like something happened to me and I can't remember what, but the whistle brings it all back."

Whoo! Whoo! It was close enough now that they could hear the wheels rolling over the steel rails.

"Maybe it sounds sad," Rambler began, " 'cause it wants all of us to get on it and get away from here and it knows we never will."

"I guess you got to ride it for all of us, Rambler. Ain't you scared to hop a train at night?"

"Night or day. It's the same train, ain't it?"

They could see the beam of the engine's light as the train came out of the curve and headed toward them. "You be good, Lucille." The train was on them now and as it started to pass, Rambler ran alongside, and when he saw an open boxcar he leaped, grabbing a rung of the car's ladder. He hung there a moment then, his feet finding the bottom rung, quickly climbed to the top. He lowered himself into the open car and put his head out. Looking down the track he thought he saw a small figure waving.

24

He knew he was imagining it, but he also knew that she was there. That he couldn't see her didn't mean she wasn't.

And the next Saturday night, he wasn't surprised when he heard himself sing:

> *I left Lucille, standing by the railroad track.*
> *I left Lucille, standing by the railroad track.*
> *She said, "Never mind the Devil,*
> *Baby, please come back."*

But he never did.

LOUIS

"Louis?"

He woke up instantly. "Who's that?"

"Shhh. It's me. Charlotte. I got to get back to the house before master finds out I'm gone. But I heard him and ol' miss talking at supper tonight. They fixing to sell you. Master say he don't want to do it, but he need the money. Say he broke. And he talk about how young and healthy you are. He say you bring a good price on the block."

"He say all that?"

"Sho' did."

"He say when he gon' sell me?"

"Soon as he can."

Neither spoke for a moment. Then Charlotte said, "I just thought I ought to tell you. I got to get back now, Louis."

Before he could thank her, Charlotte was out the door and gone. Louis didn't want to believe her. Why would master sell him? He wasn't like a lot of the niggers who were always causing trouble. He hadn't done nothing wrong. He didn't talk back and pretend like he was sick to get out of working. How come master had to sell him? He wasn't even that big. If master had to sell somebody, how come he didn't sell Lucius? He was a big nigger. He'd bring a good price. Or Mattie? She was sixteen and already had three babies. Somebody pay good money for a girl like her.

As much as it hurt him to find out that master would sell him, he didn't think Charlotte was lying. She worked right there in the house with her mother, and they were always slipping down to the slave quarter to tell what they had heard in the big house.

He sat up on the edge of the bed and wondered what to do. If his mother had been alive, she could've helped him. But she'd died that past spring and now there was no one to tell him anything. He was seventeen, but he'd always had someone to tell him what to do—his mother, the overseer, the driver, or Master Jenkins.

Charlotte had been telling him to get away that night before it was too late. But where would he go? If he got caught, not only would he be sold, he would get a beating he would remember to his grave. He wished he could've had more time to think. He didn't want to go plunging off through the woods like some who didn't know where they were going and got caught before they'd gone two miles. What would he eat? And how many days and nights would he have to be running and hiding until he came to the big river? What if it rained or the weather suddenly turned cold? The weather could drop down to freezing in almost no time in November.

Being a slave for Master Jenkins hadn't been that bad. He had never been whipped or punished. Only those who didn't obey had it hard. He heard different ones talking about how they ought to be free, and that was all right, he guessed. But he always wanted to ask somebody, How do you be free? All he knew was how to be a slave. He stood up, sighing heavily. But if he didn't want to be sold, he had to run.

He stood in the middle of the room trying to think of something to take with him that would remind him of home. But there was nothing. All he had was the shirt and pants he wore. What he really wanted was something that had belonged to his mother, but she had been put in the ground in all she had owned. For a moment he almost

cried, but he couldn't. There was no time. If he was going to go, he had to do it quickly and get far away from
the plantation before the sun came up.

He walked slowly to the door, opened it a crack, and
looked up and down the slave quarter for any sign of life.
All was still. He slipped out the door, and moving quickly,
went around to the back of the cabin and into the woods a
few hundred yards away. It was a cool night and the thin
shirt and pants he wore would not be enough if it took
him many nights to reach the big river. And he had no
idea how far away the big river was.

He came to a clearing, which he recognized as being at
the edge of the plantation. He looked at the sky. Many
nights his mother had shown him the Drinking Gourd, as
the slaves called the pattern of stars that were shaped like
a dipper. She had told him that the two stars which formed
the front part of the dipper were the pointers. If you drew
an imaginary line from them into the sky and stopped at
the first star the line came to, that was the North Star.
And if you followed that star, it would lead you to the big
river. On the other side was freedom.

He had never thought he would be following that star
one night. His mother had known, though. He looked at
the star, surprised that it was so small. It wasn't even that
bright. A star that important to a man should shine like
the one which led the Three Wise Men to the baby Jesus.

Louis looked at it until he could recognize it without

looking for the Drinking Gourd first. All the while he listened for the sound of footsteps crashing through the woods behind him. He listened too for the sound of baying hounddogs, "nigger dogs" they called them, their noses to the ground, following an invisible trail of odor that would lead to him. He heard nothing, though, except an occasional frog, the crickets, and an owl.

Crouching low, he ran across the clearing and into the woods on the other side. He kept the North Star in sight through the branches of the trees. He ran until his chest burned with pain. Then he walked until he caught his breath, only to run again until the pain once more became unbearable.

It was almost light when he stumbled out of the woods and, to his amazement, onto the bank of a big river. He hadn't thought he would come to it for many days. Maybe this wasn't the big river the slaves talked about. It looked big, however. He had never seen such a big river and couldn't imagine one being any bigger. It was brown and very wide, moving slowly like a giant stream of molasses.

He didn't know what to do. If it wasn't the big river, he was lost. But if it was the big river, it meant that all those slaves who talked about freedom every night were so close they could be free tomorrow night. He wanted to go back and tell them.

It was light enough now to see trees on the other side of the river. They didn't look any different from the trees on his side. How would he know it was free land if it looked the same as slave land? But even if it wasn't free land, he would be safer on the other side of the river.

He walked along the bank until he saw an overturned skiff. He ran to it and found a long paddle lying in the bottom. Without hesitating he pushed the skiff into the water and began rowing.

Though the river had looked slow-moving from the bank, the current was deep and strong and threatened to send him along faster than he wanted to go. He tried rowing straight across, but the water simply pushed him downstream as if he and the boat were a stick. Rowing furiously, he discovered that if he could keep the boat at an angle, he would eventually reach the other side as the river carried the boat downstream.

It seemed to take the boat forever before it touched bottom on the other side, and the sun was up now. He was sure someone had seen him, but as he leaped from the boat and looked around, he saw no one. He scrambled up the embankment quickly and into the tall grasses at the top. He lay there for quite a while, breathing heavily. He supposed he was in free land. He didn't know what he had expected, but he thought something would be different. The grass, however, felt just like the grass on the plantation. Even if it did, he told himself, he had to be in free country. He had to be! If he wasn't, he didn't know what he was going to do. He didn't even know which way to go.

All he had ever heard was "the big river." If that wasn't it, he was so lost that he would never find freedom.

He raised up and looked around. He saw that he was on the edge of a meadow or a large field. To his right were woods, and in the distance he could see the silhouette of a house. He decided to hide in the woods and make his way slowly toward the house until somebody came out. Then he would decide what to do.

He hadn't been hiding in the woods back of the house long before a black man came out the door carrying a bucket. Louis watched him lower the bucket down the well that stood a few yards from the door. He must have crossed the big river, he concluded, because no colored man would be living in a house off to itself in slave country. Yet he couldn't be sure. The man might be living out there just to help white folks get the runaways. Louis didn't know what to do and he panicked when he saw the man raise his bucket and turn back toward the house. He reached down, picked up a stone, and threw it toward the man. It landed close enough to the man that he turned and looked toward the woods. He set the bucket down and walked cautiously in Louis's direction.

As he got closer Louis saw that he was middle-aged, slight in build, with what Louis thought was a kindly face. Still Louis was afraid to step out from hiding. How did he know if he could trust the man? He didn't. But he stepped hesitantly out from behind the tree.

"You just come across?" the man said, smiling.

"Yessuh," Louis replied, moving back as the man came closer.

The man smiled. "It's all right, son. You're safe now."

Louis followed the man into the house. "My name's Thomas Miller. You have a seat," he said, pointing to a chair at the kitchen table. "Mable!" he shouted. "One more done got over."

"Hallelujah!" a voice yelled from the upstairs. "Pretty soon ol' miss be having to get out in the fields herself, now won't she?" A loud high-pitched laugh followed the remark. "I be right down."

Thomas turned to Louis. "You just make yourself at home, son," he said softly. "The woman'll be down in a minute to fix you something to eat. You must be pretty hungry."

"Yessuh. Ain't had much time to think about no food, but I guess the stomach could use a little something."

"Well, you in free land now. This here is Ohio. What do they call you?"

"Louis."

"Louis what?"

"Just Louis. My master's name is Jenkins, but my mama—she died last spring—she say not to ever use that name. But she never give me no other one."

"Well, you can pick any one you want to now. This here is Mable," he said, pointing to the woman who had just entered the room. "I'm going out and finish my chores. If there's anything you want, you just ask her."

The late-autumn-morning sun filled the room with a cold light. Mable Miller put a few small pieces of wood in the kitchen fireplace and in a minute had a fire going. As she hummed to herself, Louis knew that was how his mother would have been if she had been in free land. She liked to sing, too, but her songs were always mournful. If she had made it to freedom, she could've sung happy songs. "You free, Mrs. Miller?" he asked suddenly.

The large woman laughed. "Son, me and Thomas are runaways, just like you."

"Huh?"

She nodded her head. "That's the truth. We got away from ol' massa twenty-five years ago, but only after he had done sold all our chillun into cotton country. Most of the colored people you'll see around here are runaways, just like you. Ain't none of us been set free. We just took our freedom." She laughed. "That's right! We just took it. And ain't going to give it back either." She laughed again. "And me and Thomas done seen a many one like you come over. I guess over a thousand runaways done passed through here. Done set right there at that table like you are now. Then we sends 'em a little farther along the Road."

"You mean I can't stay here? I'd work real hard."

Mrs. Miller smiled. "I know you would, son, and I'd

love to have you stay. A boy like you need someone to look after him. But, son, it ain't safe for you here. Why, you almost sitting in you ol' massa's backyard, and before nightfall he'll probably be snooping around here looking for you. We got to get you started on your way to Canada."

"Where's that?"

"It's quite a ways from here, but once you gets there, you be under the protection of the Queen of England and, honey, she don't let nobody bother us colored folks. Not even Uncle Sam."

Louis didn't understand. He'd thought that after he crossed the big river, he would be free. But Mrs. Miller said she wasn't free. But she was. And she said he had to go to Canada, but she and Mr. Miller hadn't gone anywhere.

At breakfast he decided to ask Mr. Miller. "Mr. Miller?"

"Yes, Louis?"

"Is I free?"

Thomas smiled. "Well, yes and no. Under the law the only colored person what's free is those that got free papers saying that they was either born free or set free. The rest of us is free 'cause we say we are. We're as free as anybody else, I guess, except if my old master came up here today and wanted to take me back into slavery, I'd have to go with him, if I didn't run or kill him."

"But my mama told me that once I got across the big river I was free."

"Well, it's a funny kind of freedom us colored folks got. Let's put it this way. You're free as long as you don't get caught. I wouldn't worry about it too much. Most of the people around in these parts are friendly to runaways. The colored man has a lot of friends among the white people. Of course, there's some whites as bad as any across the river. They're always nosing around, trying to find out who's free and who ain't so they can collect the reward for sending some poor colored man or woman back into slavery. You just be careful who you make friends with and you'll be all right. If you act like you free, then you are."

"Yassuh."

After breakfast Mrs. Miller came in with an armful of women's clothes. "You have to put these on, son."

"No'm. Not me. I don't wear no women's clothes."

The Millers laughed. "You only got to wear them until we get you to a house in the city. It's a disguise. Your old master'll be looking for you, not a woman."

Louis shook his head. "I didn't bargain on putting on no women's clothes to be free."

"Being dressed like a woman don't mean you stopped being a man. Do it?"

Louis thought about it for a minute. "That's true," he concluded, "but I still don't like the idea."

Louis looked quite nice in his long gingham dress and bonnet, and Mrs. Miller took him to the home of Reverend and Mrs. Brown in the colored section of Cincinnati. The Browns greeted him warmly, though Louis was too busy taking off the dress and bonnet to pay much attention to them. Then he was suddenly tired, and Mrs. Brown took him to a small room upstairs where he lay on the bed and was asleep before she closed the door.

He was up in time for supper. She had fried a chicken that evening, and Louis had never seen so much food. It was only one chicken, but on the plantation he'd never had anything but the gizzards. Sometimes his mother made soup from the chicken feet. But those were the only parts Master Jenkins had let them have.

"Now, you just help yourself," Mrs. Brown told him. "I don't want to see a bit of that chicken left when you get up from the table."

"Yes'm."

There wasn't much conversation at dinner. Louis noticed that Reverend Brown ate as if he too had just crossed the big river. Between them they finished off the chicken quickly.

"That was a good meal, Mrs. Brown," the Reverend said. "It wasn't until I came across the river and had my first chicken that I understood why my old master didn't want us to ever have any chicken. Why, if I'd known chicken was this good, I would've probably stole every chicken on the place." He chuckled. "Ol' massa knew what he was doing when he tried to keep us niggers separated from his chickens. That's the truth."

"You a slave too?" Louis asked.

"Thirty years I was on the plantation. Been on this side for fifteen years now." He was a short, stout dark-skinned man and was the pastor of the First Baptist Church, which was next door to the house. "I come across in the wintertime. That was a fool thing to do. There was chunks of ice in that river bigger than this house. I didn't have on bit no more than you do either. But the Lord saw me through. Yes, He did. I come on here to Cincinnati, met Mrs. Brown, and married her. Then I got the call to preach and about the same time enlisted on the Road. And that's about it."

"What was the road you enlisted on?"

Reverend Brown laughed. "The Road? You on it right now."

Louis looked around. He wasn't on a road. He was sitting in Reverend Brown's kitchen. At least he thought it was.

Reverend Brown laughed louder. "It ain't no road you can see. The white folks think it goes underground, 'cause every time they come looking for one of their slaves and can't find 'em they say, "Them niggers must've gone underground." He chuckled. "It's what we call the Underground Railroad, son. Brother and Sister Miller who brought you here? Well, they part of it. Me and Mrs. Brown are too. I reckon there are a couple of thousand people all over the North who hide out runaway slaves, take 'em from place to place until they cross on over into Canada. You know that room you was sleeping in?"

Louis nodded.

"Now, that's sho' 'nuf on the Road. That's a secret room. Built it myself. Bet if you go upstairs now, you couldn't find that room to save your life. I done had white people come in this house and the very people they was looking for was upstairs in that room. White folks look everywhere and never found a soul. And when the whole matter died down, I took them slaves my own self, dressed the men in women's clothes, got a empty casket, a couple of wagons, and drove 'em out of here just like we was going to a funeral." He laughed so loud and hard that tears began to well up in his eyes. "That's the truth. Drove them runaways right through the center of town, I did, and on out to the cemetery, where we was met by another wagon that carried 'em on farther. And last thing I heard, them slaves was sitting happy in Canada."

Louis looked at Reverend Brown admiringly. "That was a mighty brave thing to do."

The Reverend shook his head. "Naw, son. I just hates slavery. That's all. And the truth of the matter is, it's a lot of fun tricking them people. I get a kick out of it every time there's a knock on my door and some runaways walk

41

in the house. I ain't doing nothing more than a lot of other people are doing. They are going to either get rid of this slavery, or we are going to run off every slave they got! And that's all there is to it."

Louis nodded.

"Well, I guess we better start making plans to get you on to Canada."

Louis looked startled. "Canada?"

"Once you up there, then you free sho' 'nuf."

"Yessuh. That's what Mrs. Miller say. But I don't know nothing about no Canada."

"This time last night you didn't know a thing about Ohio, did you?"

"Yessuh. That's true. But you and Mrs. Brown didn't go to no Canada. Y'all stayed right here. Mr. and Mrs. Miller too."

"And that's what you want to do."

"Yessuh."

"It's risky, Louis. One day you might be walking down the street and bump right into your old master. It has happened to more than one slave."

"Yessuh."

Reverend Brown didn't say anything for a while. "Well, we'll see. If your master comes looking for you and we find out about it, we won't have no choice but to pass you farther on the Road. But if he don't, then I don't see why you can't stay. Like you said, there's plenty of us here already. I guess one more won't be noticed."

Louis remained hidden at Reverend Brown's for three weeks before it was decided that he could come out. Reverend Brown found a room for him to rent with Mrs. Winter, a widow who belonged to his church.

Louis spent his first few days after leaving Reverend Brown's walking the streets. Never having been to a city, the sight and noise of the carriages and horsedrawn wagons frightened him. The sidewalks were jammed with people and he wondered if he would ever get used to all of it. He was most impressed, however, by the blacks. He stood on streetcorners and stared at the black men who were dressed better than his master dressed on Christmas. And the women! In their wide hooped dresses he thought each one was the prettiest woman he had ever seen. Ol' miss looked like po' white trash next to any one of them.

It was not long, though, before he stopped noticing the noise and crowded streets. He had to turn his mind to finding a job. All he knew was farm work, and since he couldn't read and write, there weren't too many jobs he could get. But Reverend Brown prevailed upon Joseph Stokes, a white grocer, to give Louis a job unpacking crates, putting merchandise on the shelves, and making deliveries. Stokes wasn't a part of the Underground Railroad, but he didn't have any sympathy with slavery either.

He wasn't the kind of man who would hide a runaway, but he wouldn't turn one in. He had hired blacks before at Miller's request, but they seldom stayed long. One morning they simply didn't show up for work and Mr. Stokes never asked any questions.

Louis liked working at the store. He was there when Mr. Stokes opened up in the morning and stayed until he closed at night. Each day he learned something new, even if it was nothing more than how to weigh a pound of rice.

Once a week there was a literacy class in the basement of Reverend Brown's church. Louis was never absent. They didn't have any books, so the young girl who taught the class used the Bible. Each night after work Louis went home and after supper sat in the parlor with Mrs. Winter, spelling out words from the Bible. He wondered if the day would ever come when he could read like the girl who taught the class. "That girl read like she was born with a book in her hand," Louis told Mrs. Winter one evening.

The old woman smiled. "This time last year that girl was spelling out words just like you doing now. She a slave too. Come across the river about a year and a half ago."

Louis gaped. "That the truth?"

"You calling me a liar, boy?" Mrs. Winter said sternly.

"Oh, no'm. I wouldn't do that. I just can't hardly believe it."

But by the following spring Louis was no longer spell-

44

ing words out syllable by syllable. He read the Bible aloud to Mrs. Winter each evening and could even read the newspaper without too many errors.

Besides work and study, Louis looked forward to going to church every Sunday. More than anything else, it reminded him of the plantation. There hadn't been a church there for the slaves, but they would go back in the woods and Amos would preach to them about the Hebrew children getting away from Pharaoh. Reverend Brown had a deep voice, like Amos, and when he shouted, Louis thought the windows would break. "And God sent Moses down into Egypt land, and Moses said to ol' Pharaoh: 'PHARAOH! YOU LET MY PEOPLE GO!'" Louis could see Egypt in his mind and it looked just like Master Jenkins's place, and Moses looked like Reverend Brown. Amos had preached about it too, and what little Louis had heard about freedom had come from Amos. But somehow it was better hearing about it when you knew what it was.

Other Sundays Reverend Brown preached about how black people had to improve themselves. "We can't have no lazy people. We can't have no dirty people. We can't have no foul-mouthed or drunk people. We ain't down on the plantation no more! We ain't working for ol' massa now! We working for ourselves! And if we gon' be lazy and dirty and foul-mouthed and drunk, the white people are going to say, The colored people don't know how to be free. They'll say, Let them that's in slavery stay in slavery, and these that are up here, well, come get 'em and take 'em back. They don't know how to be free!"

Louis listened intently, nodding his head in agreement. He didn't want anyone looking at him and thinking he should be a slave. Slavery was all right when he didn't know any better, but now he did. He was free and he only wished every slave was.

One Sunday afternoon he went to Reverend Brown and asked him if he could become a conductor on the Underground Railroad. "If I could do the kind of thing you and Mr. Miller do, then I'd be doing something to help break down slavery."

Reverend Brown nodded. "Well, Louis, you doing a lot as it is."

"How's that?"

"I hear a lot of folks saying what a fine example you set for the young people. And if all the runaway slaves was like you, then it would be impossible for the white man to say our people don't deserve their freedom. Just by working hard, keeping yourself neat and clean the way you do, learning all you can, you doing as much as me, Brother Miller, or anyone else."

Louis smiled and told himself that he was going to work even harder.

One afternoon about a year after he had crossed the big river, Louis was working in the back of the store when he heard a familiar voice coming from the front. He couldn't remember where he had heard the voice, but the sound of it made him smile. He started toward the door leading into the front of the store, and as he put his hand on the knob he stopped. Massa! He listened again, but there was no mistake. Master Jenkins was talking to Mr. Stokes.

He wondered how Master Jenkins had found him. Then again, maybe he hadn't. Maybe he just happened to come into the store not even thinking about him. But that didn't seem likely. He wouldn't have any reason to be in a grocery store unless he thought Louis was there.

Louis listened to the sound of the voice again but couldn't make out any words. Then he heard footsteps coming toward the storeroom. For a second he was unable to move, but as the footsteps got closer he quickly made his way to the back door and slipped into the alley. He ran down the alley until he came to the street, where he slowed down. If people saw him running up the street, they would know something was wrong. He didn't run, but walked as fast as he could to Reverend Brown's.

A week later Louis was in Columbus, Ohio. Reverend Brown had gotten him out of Cincinnati that same night to a farm ten miles away. Each night he had been moved until he was left with Reverend John Moore, a Baptist

47

minister in Columbus. He was supposed to have gone from there to Canada, but once again Louis balked at the idea. Reluctantly Reverend Moore let him stay in Columbus and found him a room in the home of Mr. and Mrs. Eli Williams, an elderly couple who belonged to his church.

Louis quickly found work for himself in another grocery store and, as in Cincinnati, his life eased into a pattern of work six days a week, church on Sundays, and every Friday night the meeting of the anti-slavery society. He looked forward to these meetings each week where the question of slavery was discussed. He was astounded to see whites at the meetings and couldn't believe it when they stood up and denounced slavery with such anger that he wondered if they had once been slaves, though he knew they couldn't have been. But even more surprising to him were the blacks who spoke as eloquently as the whites. Some of these men, he learned, had been slaves. Yet to listen to them, Louis would have thought they had attended the finest schools in the world. Sometimes he couldn't understand everything he heard, but he smiled and applauded because it sounded good and a black man had said it. He never said anything. But it never occurred to him that he should. There were men who could say everything and he was just proud that he was there to hear them.

In 1850 the anti-slavery meetings took on a note of urgency. Congress had just passed a new Fugitive Slave

Law, and blacks and anti-slavery whites were angered by it. Since the days when the Constitution was written, almost a hundred years earlier, there had been laws giving slaveowners the right to reclaim runaways, no matter where they were found. These laws had, for the most part, been ignored, and slaveowners complained that anti-slavery whites were actually making war on their rights as slaveowners by hiding and helping runaway slaves. In 1850 Congress passed a new law making it illegal for anyone to help a runaway slave. It was a law aimed directly at stopping the Underground Railroad.

In the first months following the passage of the new law, slave hunters came to many towns and cities, taking anyone they could, ex-slave or freeman. Many runaway slaves left and went farther north to Canada.

Mr. and Mrs. Williams urged Louis to leave before it was too late. He had almost been caught in Cincinnati. Louis, however, didn't think Master Jenkins would follow him all the way to Columbus. He wasn't worth all that trouble.

II

The big clock in the hallway had just finished striking ten when Estelle Williams said to her husband, "Eli, something done happened to the boy."

They were sitting in front of the fireplace, and Eli Williams lowered the Bible he had been reading and turned to her. "You think so?"

"I know so. Late as he ever come home from the store has been nine. And the clock just struck ten."

"Well, let's wait a little while longer. Maybe he ran into some friends and went to have a little drink."

"Eli Williams! You know there's a God in Heaven and you know that Louis ain't never had a drink of whiskey in his life and never would. Something done happened. I know it has."

They were silent for a moment. "Well?" Mrs. Williams finally said.

"Well, what?" He knew what she was going to say, but he didn't feel like hitching up the horse and wagon at that time of night. It was cold outside and it was almost his bedtime anyway.

"I think you better go look for him."

"Estelle, you worry over that boy like he's your own."

"Closest thing I ever had. He ain't nothing but a baby anyway."

He sighed and closed the Bible. "Awright. If you want to send me out to catch my death of cold——"

"Hush up your mouth. I ain't doing no such thing and you know it."

He chuckled. "I know. I just hates to leave this fire."

Eli Williams was almost seventy years old, though one couldn't tell it from looking at him. His walk was as firm and steady as that of a much younger man, and he could still put in a full day's hard work. But he was beginning to feel his age. He didn't get out of bed as quickly in the morning any more and he had a hard time keeping awake after supper every evening. That winter had seemed the coldest one of his life, though the thermometer hadn't gone any lower than it had in previous winters.

As he hitched the horse to the wagon, he hoped to hear Louis's voice calling from the house. Eli was dressed warmly, but the cold seemed to be coming from inside him as his growing sense of dread told him that Estelle was right. Something had happened to the boy and he didn't want to know it.

He climbed onto the wagon seat and snapped the reins. Walking the horse rapidly through the empty streets, he was at Mr. Alley's store in a few minutes. The store was dark. He took the lantern from the side of the wagon and climbed down. The street was empty. He tried the door, and finding it locked, turned to go around to the back. Then he saw it lying on the sidewalk. A shoe. Even before he stopped to pick it up he knew that it was Louis's. He'd gone with the boy to buy those shoes.

He jumped back on the wagon and with a loud "Giddap!" and a snap of the reins galloped the horse toward Mr. Alley's house. Worried now, he didn't feel the cold air pressing against him.

He pulled up at the grocer's house a short distance away.

"What brings you out this time of night, Eli?" Mr.

Alley said when he answered the rapid knock at his door.

"Sorry to bother you, Mr. Alley, but me and the old woman was wondering if you knew where Louis was."

"Louis? No. No, I don't."

"He ain't come in yet. He didn't say nothing about going somewhere tonight, did he?"

"No. I left the store around six and told him to lock up at seven. That's the last I saw him."

Eli showed him the shoe. "I found it on the sidewalk in front of the store."

Sam Alley slammed his fist into the palm of his hand. "I should've known it! I should've known it!"

"What's that, sir?"

"Last week some white man was in the store. He was a stranger and was chatting about the weather and this, that, and the other. I didn't think anything of it at the time, him being a stranger and all, but he asked me some questions about Louis. Not by name. But asked me about the boy he'd seen working there. Louis was out making a delivery at the time. I'll bet my last bag of oats that man was Louis's ol' master."

Eli nodded. "Well, thanks, Mr. Alley. I'm gon' get on over to Reverend Moore's and tell him what done happened. Maybe he'll know what to do."

Reverend Moore had just gone to bed when he heard the loud knocking at his door. He got up, thinking that it was an unexpected group of runaways. But when he saw Eli, he knew that Louis had been captured. "The only thing we can do is to send a wire to some of the good brethren in Cincinnati. Maybe they'll be able to stop them before they can get Louis back across the river."

They went down to the telegraph office at the railroad station. The telegraph operator was an agent of the Underground Railroad and quickly tapped out a message to a lawyer he knew of in Cincinnati. Once the telegraph keys were quiet, silence returned to the small room. The three men looked at each other but said nothing. Finally they left, having done all they could.

III

The sun shone brightly that Wednesday morning, and Louis sat in the courthouse in Cincinnati, wondering how it could be a sunny day when he was about to be sent back into slavery. It had been a month since that night the marshal of Columbus had grabbed him as he was locking up the store. From the minute he felt the arms around him, he knew that what he had thought couldn't happen had. He had fought with the marshal, but a blow to his head with a pistol had knocked him out.

When he regained consciousness, he found himself lying in the back of a carriage, his hands and feet tied. The marshal told him that he was being taken to Cincinnati, where Master Jenkins waited to carry him back across the big river.

"If I had my way, I wouldn't do this," the marshal told him. "But I'm a United States Marshal, and it's my job to carry out the law, no matter whether I like it or not."

Louis told himself that he would never be a marshal if that was what it meant.

As they reached the outskirts of Cincinnati, the carriage suddenly came to a stop. Louis raised up when he heard a voice tell the marshal that he was under arrest for kidnapping. Later he learned that the marshal was supposed to have taken him to a judge who would have decided if Master Jenkins had a claim on him. Instead the marshal was going to deliver him directly to Master Jenkins, and that was against the law. Louis was so happy he wanted to shout. He wasn't free, but he wasn't a slave yet either.

He felt better once he was in jail in Cincinnati. Reverend Brown and Mr. and Mrs. Miller came to see him every day. He hoped that they were going to help him break out, but they told him that there was nothing they could do. This time it was up to him, and there was nothing he could do either.

When the trial began, Louis had almost resigned himself to going back. He sat in the court and listened to the lawyer Reverend Brown had gotten for him argue why he shouldn't be returned. Master Jenkins and the marshal had their lawyer who argued why he should be. Louis never said a word. He thought it was kind of strange that everybody could have a say about what should be done to him except him. And somebody who didn't even know him was going to do the deciding. It didn't make sense. But everybody said that was the way the law worked.

It was the last morning of the trial. The courtroom was filled with people. He had never seen most of them before, but they were there, white and black. It made him feel like he was important.

The courtroom was longer than it was wide, with a table in the center. The judge and the two lawyers sat on one side of the table, and behind them stood all the blacks. Opposite the judge and the lawyers sat Louis between Master Jenkins and the marshal. Louis had always liked Master Jenkins, and even during the trial had been glad to see him. He wouldn't have minded sitting and talking with him, telling him all he had done since he'd been free. Master Jenkins didn't look like he would be interested in hearing about it though.

Behind Louis, the sheriff, and Master Jenkins the white people stood. People continued to come into the room until even the doorway was packed. There were so many people, Louis thought, a fly would've had trouble finding a place on the floor to light.

The judge had begun reading his decision. His voice was so low that even Louis, who was only on the other side of the table, could hardly hear him. Everybody leaned forward to hear better. Louis listened for a minute, but he couldn't understand a word the judge was saying. Maybe he was talking some other language.

The judge continued reading from the thick sheaf of papers he held and the crowd moved closer so as not to miss a word. People were leaning against Louis's chair and he moved back a little to try and give himself more room. He moved farther from the table than he had intended and found himself sitting almost behind Jenkins and the marshal. He started to scoot his chair forward but stopped when he realized that neither of the two men had seemed to notice anything. He looked across the table at the lawyers and the judge. They had not looked up. He looked again at Jenkins and the marshal. Their eyes were fixed on the judge.

He knew it couldn't work, but if he was going to escape, this was his last chance. He looked at Master Jenkins and the marshal again, who still didn't notice that he had moved.

Louis pushed his chair back a little more. The crowd behind him noticed what he had done and people squeezed tightly around to conceal him. He looked at the men at the table. All were listening to the judge. Louis still couldn't believe that it would work. Neither could anyone else in the room, most of whom by now had stopped listening to the judge and were looking at Louis. He thought he stopped breathing as he slowly got up out of the chair and slipped into the crowd. A hand came out of the crowd and put a hat on his head, which he immediately pulled low over his face.

No one spoke or even looked at him too intently, but people moved aside just a little to let him make his way through quickly. He eased through the crowd of whites around to the opposite side of the room where the blacks were standing. As he neared the door, he wanted to look around to see what Master Jenkins and the marshal were doing, but he didn't dare. Without a backward glance he slipped out the door and into the sunlight. He walked down the steps very slowly, up the street, and to the corner. The only place he could think of going was the black cemetery. He doubted if Master Jenkins would think to look for him in the graveyard. Too, he knew Charles, the gravedigger, who lived there. Charles would help him.

He had been gone five minutes when the marshal suddenly shouted, "He's gone!" Everyone in the courtroom burst into laughter. The marshal and Master Jenkins ran out of the courthouse, their faces red with anger and humiliation.

For several weeks they searched through Cincinnati but found no trace of Louis. They were forced to conclude that "that nigger must've gone underground." All the time, however, Louis had been in the secret room at Reverend Brown's, where he had been brought, disguised as a woman, from the gravedigger's.

The night Reverend Brown came to him and said, "Son, all the arrangements are made for you to go to Canada," Louis said, "Yessuh." Reverend Brown knew he meant it this time.

BEN

It was the spring of 1853 when I met Ben. Or at least made his acquaintance. Now, some twenty years later, I think it is presumptuous for any white man to think that he has ever really "met" a Negro. For two people to truly meet, they must trust each other, and why should a black trust a white man?

I was twenty-three at the time, just out of law school, and had accompanied my father, also a lawyer, on a business trip to New Orleans. It was my first visit to the

60

Southern states and I had looked forward to the trip with a mixture of dread and curiosity. I wondered what the South would be like, wanted to see it, and yet thought that I could never be comfortable with what I saw. Father, on the other hand, had many clients among slaveholders, went South at least once a year, and was anxious for me to meet some of them who, he assumed, would one day be my clients. He knew how I felt about slavery but never took it seriously. "You'll outgrow those feelings," he would say. "When you actually see niggers, you'll realize what a favor we're doing them by keeping them as slaves."

I saw them that spring, standing in the fields with hoes in their hands, walking along the boarded sidewalks of towns and cities, or simply standing. But I didn't know what I was seeing. Were they as mute and passive as they looked? They moved slowly, like zombies, but then I wondered if I would move any faster if my life belonged to another man. In New Orleans we chanced upon a slave auction and at that moment, at least, I knew without a doubt that selling children from their mothers could not be justified. Even Father appeared a bit unnerved by it and was as anxious to leave as I.

We spent some two months in New Orleans and its environs, and in all fairness I must say that none of the whites with whom I came into contact seemed like the devils the Northern abolitionists painted them to be. Never have I been treated with such consideration as on

61

that and my many subsequent trips south.

So nothing had really been resolved in me when we got off the train in Louisville, Kentucky. Then again, I guess something had. After all, I had just spent several months with slavery all around me and had made no effort forcibly to free one slave, something that I, in my more romantic moments, would fantasy about doing. In fact I had found it relatively easy to live with slavery, to be waited on hand and foot by silent colored servants. I had not tried to persuade one slaveholder to manumit his slaves, though I was in constant company with the gentlemen. So I guess I felt rather ashamed of myself when we stepped off the train, though I didn't realize it at the time. But that is how it is with people, isn't it? We spend our lives not really knowing what we think and feel, afraid that if we do, it may totally disrupt our lives.

The McGuire Plantation was some fifteen miles from Louisville. Father and Elliot McGuire were old friends from college and every time Father went south he ended his trip with a month or so of hunting, fishing, and relaxing at the McGuire place. I, too, was looking forward to the time we would spend there, hoping that it would give me the occasion to try and collect my impressions and thoughts of the previous months.

As we stepped from the train, a black of medium build stepped forward, grinning. "Glad to see you again, Mr.

Johnson."

Father smiled. "It's good to see you too, Ben."

"This here yo' boy?" he asked, looking at me.

Father nodded.

"Nice to make yo' acquaintance, Master," the Negro said, turning his grin at me. "Y'all go get in the buggy," he said, pointing to the horse and carriage a few yards away. "I'll get yo' luggage."

That was Ben. He was between thirty and forty years old, though no one knew exactly. He had been born and raised on the McGuire place, and he and Elliot McGuire's son, Albert, had grown up together. They were like brothers, the McGuires were fond of telling me, even though one was a free man and the other his slave. Ben's wife, Martha, was the McGuires' cook.

We had scarcely seated ourselves in the buggy when Ben came hurrying back with our luggage, and in a few minutes we were being carried through the graceful Kentucky countryside by two of the McGuires' fine horses. Elliot McGuire raised tobacco, but his first love was horses and he was known throughout the South for his thoroughbreds. And, I must say, I have never seen since then such magnificent animals. If people took as much care in having children as Elliot McGuire did in breeding horses, we would be a nation of gods. Even now I can remember sitting on the veranda of their mansion, looking out over the meadows where the animals grazed, thinking that surely there was no more peaceful or beautiful scene in the world. And at such moments I had a difficult time thinking of any arguments against slavery.

It was almost dusk when we drove up the circular drive to the big house with its gracefully fluted columns. All slaveholders, I learned, did not live on the cultural level that the McGuires did. In fact, most did not, and it is somewhat ironic that now people think all slaveholders lived in big white mansions on thousands of acres. Even Southerners, who should know better, like to think that that was how all of the South was before the war. But it wasn't. Most slaveholders lived in ordinary frame dwellings that were distinguished by neither style nor comfort. In fact the average Northern workingman lived in more comfort than most slaveowners. But I guess it is not too great a failing that a civilization, once it has declined, wants to be remembered by its few examples of magnificence and not by the all-too-ordinary norm.

Elliot McGuire was in his mid-fifties when I met him. He was an average-looking man, neither short nor tall, handsome nor ugly. He was a lawyer and a member of the Kentucky legislature. Many felt that he could have been governor, but such a responsibility would have meant time away from his horses, something to which Elliot would never give serious consideration. He was a widower, his wife having died some years before in childbirth. I sometimes got the feeling that the death of his wife had been somewhat of a relief to him, for once, when I asked him why he had never remarried, he said, laughing, "Oh, no woman wants to take second place, especially to a horse."

We stayed only two weeks that first time, but it was long enough for me to fall in love. I met Samantha that very first evening and have yet to meet a more beautiful woman. Never had I imagined that there could be a perfect woman. Yet there she was, sitting across from me at supper. Her light-brown hair was fixed in gracefully looping curls down the back of her long white dress. Her eyes were blue, like the sky at dawn. Her voice was soft and low-pitched and made all the more musical by her refined Southern accent, which softened all the harsh sounds I hate in the English language. But as I gazed at her across the table, I always returned to those eyes, for it was there that Samantha lived. Her eyes were the tongue of her soul. Charles Sumner's greatest orations on the floor of the Senate were never as eloquent as Samantha's eyes.

She was two years younger than I and one of the most courted women in the state. But she was not anxious to marry for some reason. I think because she could never imagine leaving that place, and she hadn't met a man with whom she really wanted to share it. That is, not until she met me, for Samantha and I loved each other from the moment I took her hand in mine and bowed to kiss it. Even her brother remarked a few years later that he had noticed Samantha's inability to keep her eyes off me at supper that evening. I hadn't noticed, for each time I looked at her she was either looking downward or in another direction. But after supper, when her father invited me and my father to join him in the library for a brandy and cigars, Samantha interrupted. "Oh, I had hoped to show Mr. Johnson the house after we ate." Her father acceded to her wish, and though there are few men who enjoy an after-dinner snifter of brandy and a good cigar more than I do, nothing seemed more unappealing after Samantha expressed her desire to be with me.

How quickly those two weeks went. It seemed that Ben was driving us to the station the day after we arrived, though the calendar told me differently. Samantha and I were together almost constantly. Each morning Ben had two horses saddled and waiting for us in the driveway, and after breakfast we would be off. Around lunchtime Ben would materialize with a basket lunch prepared by Martha and we would spread a tablecloth under one of the many huge oak trees at the edge of a meadow and eat. Afterward I would enjoy the brandy and a cigar Ben had been thoughtful enough to include and lie in the grass, my head in Samantha's lap. Later I would wonder what Ben would be thinking as he sat some distance away under another tree, waiting for us to finish so he could pack the dishes and remains of the lunch and return them to the house.

§ *Ben* §

"What do you think Ben thinks of us?" I asked her once.

She smiled. "I doubt if he even notices. Why should he care?"

I shrugged. "I don't know. I just wonder if he does."

"Oh, I guess if he didn't like you, he wouldn't take one of Daddy's best cigars to put in the lunch basket. Believe me, Ben wouldn't carry a lunch basket all the way out here for just anybody. In fact I can't recall him ever being so solicitous before."

I had to admit that I was flattered. I didn't know why I cared what this slave thought, but the fact that he approved of me made me feel good. "Do you think he's happy?" I asked her a little later.

"Who? Ben? He's as much a member of the family as I am. Maybe even more so because he and Martha run that house. You Northerners don't realize just what tyrants our so-called slaves can be. Ben and Martha run this plantation as much as Father and Albert do. In fact much more than Father, because he leaves everything to Albert. And Albert leaves it all to Ben."

"Really?"

She laughed. "I guess that doesn't quite fit your idea of slaveholding, does it?"

I shook my head. "No, I guess not."

"Well, Ben can read and write. He keeps the books, decides when to sell the tobacco and for how much. Plus, when I was growing up, he used to turn me over his knee and give me a spanking every once in a while."

I laughed. "And your father didn't object?"

"Well, somebody had to do it and he knew he wouldn't."

Still, I couldn't help wondering about Ben. Maybe he was a member of the family. Nonetheless he was a slave. He was the first person I saw each morning, as he came in my room to wake me and ask me what clothes I wanted to wear that day. While I was getting out of bed, he would pour heated water into a pan for me to wash with and lay out the clothes I had indicated. When I came down to breakfast, there he was again, serving the table, and after breakfast the two horses would be waiting in the driveway, Ben holding them by their reins. He seemed to be everywhere, yet never did he look tired or in any way unhappy. Sometimes when Samantha and I were out riding, I would see him from a distance, exercising a horse. The McGuires were famous for racing horses as well as show animals, and Ben trained both. Other times, when we went near the tobacco fields, I would see him there, talking with Albert or one of the slaves. At night he was the last person I saw, as he went to turn back my bed-covers when I started up the stairs. Where he slept I never really knew. I presumed it was in the slave quarter, which was some way from the house and separated from it by a grove of trees. Though I was often curious to see it, somehow I never did.

After that first visit I returned to the McGuire Plantation as often as I could. It was never as often as I would have liked. I always went in the spring for several weeks and at Thanksgiving, generally staying over through New Year. Everyone assumed that Samantha and I would marry and it was only a question of when. As my father's associate in the law firm, I was beginning to achieve a reputation in and around Chicago and I looked forward to a respectable and prosperous career. All I needed to assure that was an attractive wife, one who could be a gracious hostess and who could carry on an intelligent conversation. Samantha was more than adequate on both accounts.

It was on my third visit, the fall of the following year, that we began to talk of marriage. There was no doubt that we should marry. We made the other feel more alive than either of us had ever thought it possible to feel. So we talked of marriage and I tried to paint her a picture of what our life would be like together in Chicago. But I had scarcely started when she interrupted me with, "But, David. I thought you would move here."

I blinked, for the thought had never occurred to me. "But what would I do?" I asked.

"Well, you could help Father and Albert with the plantation. I know they would welcome it. Albert really doesn't enjoy being a plantation owner, you know. And if it weren't for Ben, I really don't know what we would do.

Father is only interested in his horses, but he needs Ben to train them. Albert isn't that good a manager. I mean, he doesn't know how to handle the slaves. And that leaves poor Ben. Father worries sometimes about what will happen to the place when he dies. It would ease his mind so much if he knew you were going to be in charge."

We were sitting in the library in front of the fireplace. It was a chilly December evening. First frost had come that morning, and though there were still a few more warm days to come, winter had arrived. I gazed at the logs burning in the fireplace, not sure what to say. It had never occurred to me that I would have to move to Kentucky to have Samantha for a wife. And I told her so.

"But it's a good idea, isn't it?" she replied.

I said that it was, afraid to tell her that I didn't like the idea of being a slaveowner. I knew it was foolish to feel that way and that once I told my father, he would be furious, which he was. "You mean to say that you would pass up the opportunity to be one of the wealthiest and most influential men in the state of Kentucky and perhaps the nation? Not to mention having one of the most beautiful women you'll ever find for a wife? And all because you don't want to own niggers!" He raised his voice to its courtroom volume, which was loud enough to threaten to make the statue of Justice take off her blindfold to see what was going on. "What did your mother and I raise? A man or a jackass?" Mother said little,

70

§ *Ben* §

which was typical. If she ever disagreed with Father, I never knew about it. So I was left to struggle with Father alone.

Mainly, though, the struggle was with myself. What was wrong with me? I wouldn't be the first person to own slaves. And as long as one treated them humanely, what was wrong with slavery? Ben would have still been running around in the jungle with nothing on if it wasn't for slavery. Surely even he would not have preferred that. I tried every way I knew to convince myself, but something in me wouldn't be convinced.

Samantha was adamant. She would never leave the plantation. It was her home, and home seems to mean more to Southerners than it does to us Northerners. She was a part of that land and I myself couldn't imagine her anywhere else. Some mornings when I woke up I would tell myself yes! Then a few minutes later I would remember Ben, who had just left the room. And my yes became less certain.

"But Ben likes you!" Samantha protested when I tried to explain to her.

"How can I be sure?"

"What do you mean?" She was genuinely perplexed.

"I mean, how can I be sure he *really* likes me when he isn't free to know himself whether or not he likes me? He's a slave, Samantha. Part of his job is to make me think that he likes me."

71

She laughed. "Are you afraid he's going to sneak up the stairs and slit your throat one night?" she said in a teasing whisper.

I flushed. "No. No, of course not."

She laughed louder. "David! You're priceless. Simply priceless. You don't know the first thing about niggers, but when you do, you'll find out that they don't think like that. Ben doesn't think the way you do. He simply doesn't."

I wasn't sure. I couldn't convince myself that Ben didn't think, even once, that he should own the plantation. After all, he had to know that there wouldn't have been one without him. And knowing that, how was it possible for him to be content to be a slave. He ran that plantation better than many white men could have. Yet every time I observed him I could see nothing. It was as if he had buried his real self somewhere deep in his black skin. Maybe it would stay buried forever. But maybe one day it would rise from its grave. And what then?

From the beginning I had tried to talk with him. But I seldom got more than a "yes, suh" and "no, suh." He would talk freely about horses, which he loved as much as Elliot did. But about himself, nothing. Maybe Samantha was right. Maybe he didn't have any feelings about being a slave. He had never known anything else. How could he have feelings? He did, though. I knew he did, but I could never prove it.

It was the following spring when the telegraph message came, announcing the sudden death of Elliot McGuire. I left that very same day, and when I arrived several days later, Ben met me at the station.

"How is Miss Samantha, Ben?"

"She's bearing up well, sir. Better than Mr. Albert."

"What do you mean?"

"Just that he's taking it kind of hard. He's the master now, but he don't want to be."

"But everyone knows who really runs the plantation," I said.

"Yes, suh. Mr. Elliot did."

I started to tell Ben that he didn't have to pretend with me. Everyone knew that Elliot hadn't known one kind of tobacco from another. Instead I asked, "What do you mean?"

"Nothing."

I guess I had tried to probe a little too much, for he said nothing else and neither did I. But I got the feeling from him that now that Elliot McGuire was dead, there would be some kind of change. And for some reason I felt the same. Although Elliot had known little or nothing about tobacco, it had been his presence there that had made it all possible. Without him, no one knew. Albert was not the measure of his father. Not that he was bad. He wasn't. But he seemed to lack his father's love for the land, horses, and even the house itself. Elliot knew how to appreciate good brandy and always took great pains to have the best in his house. Albert, on the other hand, regarded brandy with the same attitude as he would a glass of water. It was often a joy to watch Elliot McGuire sniff a good cigar. He made you enjoy your own cigar more because he truly enjoyed his. But I couldn't say that I had ever seen Albert enjoy anything. I had never seen him hurt or be mean to anything either. But a man who enjoyed nothing was a man to be feared. By the time we drove up to the house, I was deeply worried.

As Ben had said, Samantha was well. She accepted her father's death with the dignity of her father. At supper I saw Albert, who said that he wanted to speak with me immediately after. I had been looking forward to a walk in the moonlight with Samantha, but I didn't protest. Albert had never expressed a desire to speak with me before, so it must be important.

After the meal we went into the library and he offered me one of his late father's cigars.

"When are you and Samantha getting married?" he asked abruptly. "I know that if my father hadn't died so suddenly, it would have been his wish that the two of you marry as soon as possible. He approved highly of you."

"I'm grateful. I admired him tremendously."

"I trust you will forgive me for butting into your personal life like this, but I would be greatly relieved to know that you were going to be running things around here."

"Me?" I said, feigning surprise. "I think you're much more capable than I. I'm a big-city lawyer, not a gentleman farmer. And after all, you've been running the place for many years now."

"And hating every minute of it. I don't look forward to having all of this responsibility on me," he said, stretching out his arms wearily. "Two hundred and fifty niggers to worry about. And tobacco is one of the most difficult crops in the world. You have to treat it with as much care and patience as you do a nigger." He shook his head. "No, David. The happiest day of my life will be the day you move in. You and Ben will get along fine together."

Since he had mentioned his childhood friend, I tried, as casually as I could, to see if I could learn anything about him. "What's Ben like?"

"Ben? Well, we grew up together, you know. We learned to ride at the same time. We used to wrestle, climb trees, go swimming in the river. We did just about everything together." He smiled. "It was fun in those days. But as we got older I went away to school, and Ben became Father's right hand. Sometimes we sit down and talk about how much fun we had together as kids."

He talked for some time more about his childhood friend and I was left with the impression that whatever relationship he'd had with Ben had stopped when they reached twelve years of age. It was apparent that Albert had a lot of feeling for Ben and Ben for him. But it was based on memory, not on anything that existed between them now.

"So when shall we plan for the wedding?"

"Samantha and I will talk it over and let you know."

"Good!" he said, getting up. "Once you're settled in and have learned what little I can teach you, I think I'll be off for one of your Northern cities. After all these years I just don't think I'm a country boy. You can have your horses, your meadows, and your running brooks. I'll settle for Chicago or Philadelphia."

So my mind was made up for me. It seemed that I had no choice but to become a slaveowner. I wanted to marry Samantha. Of that I had no doubt. But I was also marrying a plantation and there was no point at which I could separate her from that place. To marry her was to marry that fine Kentucky bluegrass, those tobacco fields, the stable of horses, and two hundred and fifty slaves. I had learned to manage a horse. I presumed I could learn to manage a slave, too.

We set the date for Christmas, but it was in the middle of the summer when I got a letter from Samantha telling me that Ben had run away. My impulse was to leave for Louisville immediately, but I was needed in Chicago, having several important cases to prepare for. And I realized that I simply couldn't drop everything because a nigger had run away. But Ben wasn't a nigger. He was Ben. He was a McGuire, it suddenly struck me, and yet he wasn't. That must have been what Ben had had to live with all these years. While Elliot McGuire lived, perhaps it hadn't mattered. Or maybe it had, but it had taken Elliot's death to push Ben. I didn't know. But something had made Ben rise from his grave.

I wrote Samantha immediately, asking for details, but I never got them. She wasn't the best correspondent in the world, and when she did write, her letters were generally much too brief for my romantic soul. I had accustomed myself to their brevity and infrequency, however; so it wasn't until I went down at Thanksgiving that I learned the full story.

To my surprise, she met me at the station.

"Since Ben ran away, I haven't bothered to replace him. Too, I thought you would want to see a familiar face here, and whose better than mine?"

I laughed. "Indeed. Whose?"

We chatted for the first few miles, then fell silent. It was a strange silence, though. It wasn't the silence of spring days and birds singing. It was more like the silence of autumn, with frost and cold hiding behind the reds and yellows of the leaves. Samantha and I had never been that way with each other. I asked her what was wrong.

She frowned. "Somehow, Father took it all with him."

"What do you mean?"

"I don't know, David. I just know that whatever the McGuire Plantation was, he took it with him."

When we arrived, I noticed nothing different. From Samantha's mood on the ride I expected to find the place gone to ruin. But the grass was neatly cut. The trees were as stately as ever. It still looked like the McGuire Plantation, down to the horses I saw grazing in the meadow. As I have since learned, however, a place is not just grass and buildings. It is people and memories, and how true that must have been for Samantha.

As we got out of the buggy Albert was leaving the house, a rifle in his hand. As it was near dusk, I couldn't imagine what he might be going hunting for. He greeted me warmly, saying, "It's good to see you, David. We must sit and talk very first thing tomorrow. Now, please excuse me."

As Albert walked away Samantha said, "I'm afraid you'll have to carry your own bags."

I smiled. "Oh, I daresay it's not an unwelcome change. I could never get over the feeling that I should have been carrying them anyway."

It didn't take me long to unpack and wash for dinner. When I came down, I noticed that someone other than Martha brought the food from the kitchen to the table. "Is Martha ill?" I asked Samantha.

She shook her head. "Let's eat. I'll bring you up to date after supper."

We ate quietly, chatting about inconsequential things. Such reserve was not typical of Samantha, whose joy at

78

living generally bubbled from her in a constant stream of words, jokes, and laughter. I ate quickly, anxious to know all that had transpired since I had last been there. Samantha, however, did not hurry, and it was more than an hour later when we settled ourselves in the library, in front of the warmth of the fireplace. She poured me a snifter of brandy and offered me a cigar.

Finally, "It began when Albert hired the overseer."

"Overseer?"

She nodded. "Never in the history of the McGuire Plantation have we had an overseer. Father would never have dreamed of it. At least not as long as Ben was alive. But for some reason Albert didn't trust Ben. Too, I think maybe he resented the fact that Ben knew more about the plantation than he ever would. Not that Albert ever took much interest in it. Nonetheless, it annoyed him that anytime he wanted to know anything, he had to ask Ben. At first he tried to do things himself, but he did them wrong and Ben would have to correct him. Albert felt that Ben was getting a little beside himself now that Father was dead. So he hired an overseer to take over all of Ben's duties and made Ben go to work in the fields."

"My God!" I exclaimed. "But how could he? Didn't he and Ben grow up like brothers?"

"Oh, that stopped when they were twelve. I'm sure they still like each other, but Ben was a slave. And you can't treat a slave as an equal, even if he is like your brother.

79

But I will agree that you don't treat him completely like a slave either."

"Particularly not one who had been running things."

She nodded. "The overseer Albert hired was a poor white from near here and he dearly loved to use the whip— as most of his kind do. Never once, to my knowledge, had one of our slaves felt the lash, and all pandemonium broke loose when the overseer came. Slaves began running away in droves. In a single night twelve ran away. This only infuriated Albert the more. He accused Ben of plotting against him. And I was there when Ben looked at him and said, "Mr. Albert. The whip is the plotter." But Albert thought the slaves needed to be taught a lesson. They had had it too easy, he said. This was a plantation, not a resort, and on and on and on he would go, with the overseer backing him up all the way.

"Well, the number of slaves running away became such a problem that Albert had to start patrolling the grounds at night. That's where he was going with the rifle when you came in. We never needed patrols before. Father always thought that a man with a rifle was more of a challenge to a slave than anything else. Well, one day the overseer decided that if he could break Ben, there would be no more problems with the other slaves. He was as convinced as Albert was that Ben was behind all the trouble. Oh, David, you have no idea. Tools were being broken constantly. The barn was set afire. Some of the mules had their legs broken. Everything imaginable was happening around here.

"Anyway, the overseer called Ben out of the fields and proceeded to give him a lashing. I happened to be riding that afternoon and saw it. Ben stood there, David, and never uttered a sound as that whip came down across his bare chest. He didn't move. He didn't flinch. And his flesh was a mass of blood. I was furious and rode over and stopped the overseer. He wanted to use his whip on me, but he didn't dare.

"I offered to take Ben to the house and fix his wounds, but he wouldn't let me. He simply walked off. When Albert heard what I had done, he was fit to be tied. The overseer had threatened to quit if I interfered with him once more, and I told Albert that if I saw or even heard of the overseer laying a whip to Ben again, he'd better quit, because I would take a whip to him. And I meant it."

And I knew she did. But I couldn't understand why she had gotten herself so worked up over it. I agreed that she was right to break up the whipping, but to set herself up as Ben's protector was a little much, I thought. But I didn't say anything.

"That night, oh, about two in the morning, I guess, Albert was patrolling down at the edge of the meadow. Near the stand of pin oaks. He heard a noise and called out. It was a stormy night with much thunder and lightning. And by the light of a flash of lightning, he saw Ben coming toward him, a club in his hand. He pointed his rifle at Ben and Ben told him to shoot if he wanted to, but one way or the other he was leaving that night. He said he wasn't going to stay where an overseer would put the whip to him. Albert told him that he couldn't leave and that if he tried, he would shoot him. But before he could do a thing, Ben knocked the rifle from his hands and hit him on the head with the club, knocking him unconscious.

"Then, instead of making his escape, he picked Albert up and brought him here to the house. He could've left him lying in the meadow. But he brought him here and woke me up. I asked him what was wrong, wondering what he was doing in the house at that time of night. By now it was really storming outside and the rain was coming down in sheets. He said there was someone in the library to see me and then he left. I wondered who would be coming to see me at this time of night in such weather, and for a moment I wondered if I wasn't walking downstairs to be grabbed by a group of angry slaves. But all I found was Albert lying on this couch. When I saw him, I still had no idea what had happened. I thought Ben had found Albert outside, unconscious, and brought him here. It was some hours before Albert regained consciousness and told me what I've just told you. By that time, of course, Ben was miles away, having taken his favorite stallion."

"Weren't you afraid when Ben came in your room?" I interrupted.

"Oh, he didn't come in. He knocked on the door and we talked through the door. I didn't even see him. If I had, I might have been able to read something on his face. But even if he had come into the room, I wouldn't have been afraid of Ben. The overseer, yes. But not Ben.

"Well, anyway, when the slaves discovered Ben was gone, there was nothing anyone could do. As long as Ben was here, I guess they felt they had some chance of being treated fairly. But the day the overseer whipped Ben I sensed that he had done the one thing that would eventually drive all the slaves away. Because if he whipped Ben, then it meant he would do anything. And the slaves simply waited to see what Ben would do. If he had accepted the whipping, I think things would have quieted down. But Ben did the only thing he could. He left. And whatever part of the plantation my father didn't take to the grave, Ben took that night."

"My God, Samantha! Why didn't you write and tell me all this?"

"What could you have done?"

"Well, Albert was very anxious for me to take charge and I would have done so had I known things had reached such a sorry point."

"Oh, I thought about it, but I didn't think there was anything you could do."

83

She was probably right. My intentions would have been good, but what did I know about managing a plantation? And although I was willing to try and be a slaveholder because of my love for her, I knew how much that grated against something deep in me. I didn't want to have to decide what slaves to buy and what slaves to sell, if it ever came to that. I didn't want to have to wonder if a slave was really ill or just feigning. I could manage a stable of horses, but I just couldn't believe that slaves were animals. They had human form, albeit one I found quite ugly to look upon. I would rather have been a poor white man any day than the much-talked-about Frederick Douglass. Nonetheless, as low as they were on the human scale, I couldn't shake the feeling that they, too, were human.

"Let me finish," Samantha said quietly.

"You mean there's more?"

She smiled. "Oh, the best is yet to come."

I got up and poured myself some more brandy and then sat back down. "Let's hear it," I said wearily.

"About a month after Ben ran away, he returned."

"What?"

"Once again it was in the middle of the night and Albert heard these noises coming from the woods. He called out and a voice shouted 'Don't shoot.' Albert said he recognized it immediately. Ben came out of the woods and threw himself on his knees before Albert, begging forgiveness. He said he had had such a hard time in the free states and was sorry that he had ever run off. He promised never to do it again if Albert would spare his life.

"Albert, of course, had no intention of killing him, but he decided that Ben nonetheless needed punishing. So he had him bound hand and foot and locked up for about six weeks. I thought it interesting, though, that he didn't whip him. Well, one day Ben was released and put back in the fields. Ben was a model slave and Albert and the overseer were very pleased with themselves until the morning they got up and found not only Ben gone, but Martha with him." She broke out laughing. "Then it was so obvious that Ben had got up North and had started missing Martha. So he came all the way back and did a job of acting that Mr. Booth himself would have been proud of. And just when everyone relaxed, he took Martha and got away for the second time." She laughed again. "You should've seen Albert's face that morning. He was so depressed that he didn't even give chase. I guess he didn't want to risk trying to catch Ben and failing. I was so happy, David! I bet even Father got a good chuckle out of it."

"You didn't mind?"

"Mind! I was furious at him for coming back. It almost broke my heart to see Ben going around like some whipped puppy. I almost took a whip to him myself. The morning I woke up and found that he and Martha were gone was the happiest morning of my life!"

The following day I rode around the plantation and in daylight could see clearly that it was declining. Buildings needed whitewashing. Doors needed repairing. Tools were rusting in the corners of the sheds. There were still enough slaves around to do the work. So why wasn't it being done? It was clear that Elliot McGuire had been a master of slave management. He and Ben, that is. Together they had made the slaves take pride in their work. Now it was obvious that they didn't care and no matter how many times the whip was laid against their naked backs, it would make little difference. The McGuire Plantation was dying.

I talked with Albert that morning and he told me that things weren't as bad as they might seem. He was still looking forward to Samantha's and my wedding and my coming to stay there permanently. I thanked him and said nothing, but I had changed my mind. I hadn't been aware of it then, but it had changed while Samantha was talking the night before. I think it was when she laughed. She was happy that Ben had made a fool of her and her brother. I was too, I guess, but a part of me was indignant. After all, who did Ben think he was?

It was Samantha who proposed that she move to Chicago. There was no longer any reason to remain at the plantation, and I was glad that I had not had to persuade her to leave. We were married at Christmas and came back to Chicago, where we began what has turned out to

86

be a very happy marriage. The plantation limped along under Albert's management, but we never went back. I proposed it once, but Samantha simply said no. We talked of it often, but it was the plantation of those years before her father died. Through friends we heard that it had burned to the ground during the war, and her only comment was that she hoped the horses had escaped. Albert was killed in the war, we heard, and afterward, I sold a good part of the land, retaining the meadow and the spot where the house had been, thinking that one day we would build a simple house there for our later years. And maybe we will. Samantha has begun talking of going down to see the place.

Several summers after we were married we took a vacation trip to Canada. And while we were in Toronto, we happened to take a meal at one of the hotel dining rooms. We had scarcely seated ourselves when the colored waiter appeared to take our order, and Samantha broke into laughter. I didn't know what had set her off until I looked at the waiter. "Ben!" I exclaimed.

"I beg your pardon, sir?" He looked at me without expression.

"You are Ben, aren't you?"

"You must have me confused with someone else. Timothy Fredericks is the name."

By this time Samantha was almost beside herself with laughter. She looked at him and, gasping, said, "Benjamin McGuire, don't you dare stand there and tell that lie."

Finally, when he was convinced that we had not come purposely searching for him, he smiled and told us how good it was to see us. We spent the evening with him and Martha at their home. They seemed to be doing quite well. She cooked at the hotel and he waited tables and managed the dining room. When asked, he confirmed what Samantha had believed about his return being solely for the purpose of getting Martha. None of us had much desire to reminisce, but I did ask Ben the question that had been bothering me all those years. "Were you happy as a slave, Ben? Before Elliot McGuire's death I mean?"

"Would you have been if you were me?" he replied. Then, very quietly, he added, "Massa."

I blushed with humiliation and anger, surprised that my impulse was to strike him for making me appear to be a fool. I looked at him, hoping to see the old servile smile crease his lips. Instead, I met his hard, unflinching eyes. And knowing that Ben would have liked nothing better than to have seen me dead all those years, I left, a smiling Samantha reluctantly going with me.

THE MAN WHO WAS A HORSE

It wasn't noon yet, but the sun had already made the Texas plains hotter than an oven. Bob Lemmons pulled his wide-brimmed hat tighter to his head and rode slowly away from the ranch.

"Good luck, Bob!" someone yelled.

Bob didn't respond. His mind was already on the weeks ahead. He walked his horse slowly, being in no particular hurry. That was one thing he had learned early. One didn't capture a herd of mustang horses in a hurry. For all he knew, a mustang stallion might have been watching him at that very moment, and if he were galloping, the stallion might get suspicious and take the herd miles away.

Bob looked around him, and as far as he could see the land was flat, stretching unbroken like the cloudless sky over his head until the two seemed to meet. Nothing appeared to be moving except him on his horse, but he knew that a herd of mustangs could be galloping near the horizon line at that moment and he would be unable to see it until it came much closer.

He rode north that day, seeing no sign of mustangs until close to evening, when he came across some tracks. He stopped and dismounted. For a long while he stared at the tracks until he was able to identify several of the horses. As far as he could determine, it seemed to be a small herd of a stallion, seven or eight mares, and a couple of colts. The tracks were no more than three days old and he half expected to come in sight of the herd the next day or two. A herd didn't travel in a straight line, but ranged back and forth within what the stallion considered his territory. Of course, that could be the size of a county. But Bob knew he was in it, though he had not seen a horse.

He untied his blanket from behind the saddle and laid it out on the ground. Then he removed the saddle from the horse and hobbled the animal to a stake. He didn't want a mustang stallion coming by during the night and stealing his horse. Stallions were good at that. Many times he had known them to see a herd of tame horses and, for who knew what reason, become attracted to one mare and cut her out of the herd.

He took his supper out of the saddlebags and ate slowly as the chilly night air seemed to rise from the very plains that a few short hours before had been too hot for a man to walk on. He threw the blanket around his shoulders, wishing he could make a fire. But if he had, the smell of woodsmoke in his clothes would have been detected by any herd he got close to.

After eating he laid his head back against his saddle and covered himself with his thick Mexican blanket. The chilliness of the night made the stars look to him like shining slivers of ice. Someone had once told him that the stars were balls of fire, like the sun, but Bob didn't feel them that way. But he wasn't educated, so he wouldn't dispute with anybody about it. Just because you gave something a name didn't mean that that was what it actually was, though. The thing didn't know it had that name, so it just kept on being what it thought it was. And as far as he was concerned, people would be better off if they tried to know a thing like it knew itself. That was the only way he could ever explain to somebody how he was able to bring in a herd of wild horses by himself. The way other people did it was to go out in groups of two and three and run a herd until it almost dropped from exhaustion.

He guessed that was all right. It worked. But he couldn't do it that way. He knew he wouldn't want anybody running him to and fro for days on end, until he hardly knew up from down or left from right.

Even while he was still a slave, he'd felt that way about mustangs. Other horses too. But he had never known anything except horses. Born and raised on a ranch, he had legally been a slave until 1865, when the slaves in Texas were freed. He had been eighteen at the time and hadn't understood when Mr. Hunter had come and told him that he was free. That was another one of those words, Bob thought. Even as a child, when his father told him he was a slave, he'd wondered what he meant. What did a slave look like? What did a slave feel like? He didn't think he had ever known. He and his parents had been the only colored people on the ranch and he guessed it wasn't until after he was "freed" that he saw another colored person. He knew sometimes, from the names he heard the cowboys use, that his color somehow made him different. He heard them talking about "fighting a war over the nigger," but it meant nothing to him. So when Mr. Hunter had told him he was free, that he could go wherever he wanted to, he nodded and got on his horse and went on out to the range to see after the cattle like he was supposed to. He smiled to himself, wondering how Mr. Hunter had ever gotten the notion that he couldn't have gone where he wanted.

A few months after that he brought in his first herd of mustangs. He had been seeing the wild horses since he could remember. The first time had been at dusk one day. He had been playing near the corral when he happened to look toward the mesa and there, standing atop it, was a lone stallion. The wind blew against it and its mane and tail flowed in the breeze like tiny ribbons. The horse stood there for a long while; then, without warning, it suddenly wheeled and galloped away. Even now Bob remembered how seeing that horse had been like looking into a mirror. He'd never told anyone that, sensing that they would perhaps think him a little touched in the head. Many people thought it odd enough that he could bring in a herd of mustangs by himself. But, after that, whenever he saw one mustang or a herd, he felt like he was looking at himself.

One day several of the cowboys went out to capture a herd. The ranch was short of horses and no one ever thought of buying horses when there were so many wild ones. He had wanted to tell them that he would bring in the horses, but they would have laughed at him. Who'd ever heard of one man bringing in a herd? So he watched them ride out, saying nothing. A few days later they were back, tired and disgusted. They hadn't even been able to get close to a herd.

That evening Bob timidly suggested to Mr. Hunter that he be allowed to try. Everyone laughed. Bob reminded them that no one on the ranch could handle a horse like he could, that the horses came to him more than anyone else. The cowboys acknowledged that that was true, but it was impossible for one man to capture a herd. Bob said nothing else. Early the next morning he rode out alone, asking the cook to leave food in a saddlebag for him on the fence at the north pasture every day. Three weeks later the cowboys were sitting around the corral one evening and looked up to see a herd of mustangs galloping toward them, led by Bob. Despite their amazement, they moved quickly to open the gate and Bob led the horses in.

That had been some twenty years ago, and long after Bob left the Hunter Ranch he found that everywhere he went he was known. He never had trouble getting a job, but capturing mustangs was only a small part of what he did. Basically he was just a cowboy who worked from sunrise to sunset, building fences, herding cattle, branding calves, pitching hay, and doing everything else that needed to be done.

Most cowboys had married and settled down by the time they reached his age, but Bob had long ago relinquished any such dream. Once he'd been in love with a Mexican girl, but her father didn't want her to marry a "nigger." Bob had been as confused as ever at being labeled that. He would never know what that word meant to old José. But whatever it was, it was more than enough for him to stop Pilár from marrying Bob. After that he decided not to be in love again. It wasn't a decision he'd ever regretted. Almost every morning when he got up and looked at the sky lying full and open and blue, stretching toward forever, he knew he was married to something. He wanted to say the sky, but it was more than that. He wanted to say everything, but he felt that it was more than that, too. How could there be more than everything? He didn't know, but there was.

The sun awakened him even before the first arc of its roundness showed over the horizon. He saddled his horse and rode off, following the tracks he had discovered the previous evening. He followed them west until he was certain they were leading him to the Pecos River. He smiled. Unless it was a herd traveling through, they would come to that river to drink every day. Mustangs never went too far from water, though they could go for days without a drop if necessary. The Pecos was still some distance ahead, but he felt his horse's body quiver slightly, and she began to strain forward against his tight hold on the reins. She smelled the water.

"Sorry, honey. But that water's not for you," he told the horse. He wheeled around and galloped back in the direction of the ranch until he came to the outermost edge of what was called the west pasture. It was still some miles from the ranch house itself, and today Bob couldn't see any cattle grazing up there.

But on the fence rail enclosing the pasture was a saddlebag filled with food. Each day one of the cowboys would bring a saddlebag of food up there and leave it for him. He transferred the food to his own saddlebags. He was hungry but would wait until evening to eat. The food had to have time to lose its human odor, an odor that mustangs could pick out of the slightest breeze. He himself would not venture too close to the horses for another few days, not until he was certain that his own odor had become that of his horse.

He rode southward from the pasture to the banks of the Nueces River. There he dismounted, took the saddle off his horse, and let her drink her fill and wade in the stream for a while. It would be a few days before she could drink from the Pecos. The mustangs would have noticed the strange odor of horse and man together, and any good stallion would have led his mares and colts away. The success of catching mustangs, as far as Bob was concerned, was never to hurry. If necessary he would spend two weeks getting a herd accustomed to his distant presence once he was in sight of them.

He washed the dust from his face and filled his canteen. He lay down under a tree, but its shade didn't offer much relief from the heat of high noon. The day felt like it was on fire and Bob decided to stay where he was until the sun began its downward journey. He thought Texas was probably the hottest place in the world. He didn't know, not having traveled much. He had been to Oklahoma, Kansas, New Mexico, Arizona, and Wyoming on cattle drives. Of all the places, he liked Wyoming the most, because of the high mountains. He'd never seen anything so high. There were mountains in Texas, but nothing like that. Those mountains just went up and up and up until it seemed they would never stop. But they always did, with snow on the top. After a few days though he wasn't sure that he did like the mountains. Even now he wasn't sure. The mountains made him feel that he was penned in a corral, and he was used to spaces no smaller than the sky. Yet he remembered Wyoming with fondness and hoped that some year another cattle drive would take him there.

The heat had not abated much when Bob decided to go north again and pick up his trail. He would camp close to the spot where his mare had first smelled the Pecos. That was close enough for now.

In the days following, Bob moved closer to the river until one evening he saw the herd come streaming out of the hills, across the plain, and to the river. He was some distance away, but he could see the stallion lift his head and sniff the breeze. Bob waited. Although he couldn't know for sure, he could feel the stallion looking at him, and for a tense moment Bob didn't know if the horse would turn and lead the herd away. But the stallion lowered his head and began to drink and the other horses came down to the river. Bob sighed. He had been accepted.

The following day he crossed the river and picked up

the herd's trail. It was not long after sunrise before he saw them grazing. He went no closer, wanting only to keep them in sight and, most important, make them feel his presence. He was glad to see that after a moment's hesitation, the stallion went back to grazing.

Bob felt sorry for the male horse. It always had to be on guard against dangers. If it relaxed for one minute, that just might be the minute a nearby panther would choose to strike, or another stallion would challenge him for the lead of the herd, or some cowboys would throw out their ropes. He wondered why a stallion wanted the responsibility. Even while the horses were grazing, Bob noticed that the stallion was separate, over to one side, keeping a constant lookout. He would tear a few mouthfuls of grass from the earth, then raise his head high, looking and smelling for danger.

At various times throughout the day Bob moved a few hundred yards closer. He could see it clearly now. The stallion was brown, the color of the earth. The mares and colts were black and brown. No sorrels or duns in this herd. They were a little smaller than his horse. But all mustangs were. Their size, though, had nothing to do with their strength or endurance. There was no doubt that they were the best horses. He, however, had never taken one from the many herds he had brought in. It wasn't that he wouldn't have liked one. He would have, but for him to have actually ridden one would have been like taking a piece of the sky and making a blanket. To ride with them when they were wild was all right. But he didn't think any man was really worthy of riding one, even though he brought them in for that purpose.

By the sixth day he had gotten close enough to the herd that his presence didn't attract notice. The following day he moved closer until he and his mare were in the herd itself. He galloped with the herd that day, across the plain, down to the river, up into the hills. He observed the stallion closely, noting that it was a good one. The best stallions led the herd from the rear. A mare always led from the front. But it was only at the rear that a stallion could guard the herd and keep a mare from running away. The stallion ran up and down alongside the herd, biting a slow mare on the rump or ramming another who threatened to run away or to bump a third. The stallion was king, Bob thought, but he worked. It didn't look like much fun.

He continued to run with the herd a few days more. Then came the crucial moment when, slowly, he would begin to give directions of his own, to challenge the stallion in little ways until he had completely taken command of the herd and driven the stallion off. At first he would simply lead the herd in the direction away from the one the stallion wanted to go, and just before the stallion became enraged, he would put it back on course. He did this many times, getting the stallion confused as to whether or not there was a challenger in his midst. But enough days of it and the stallion gradually wore down, knowing that something was happening, but unable to understand what. When Bob was sure the herd was in his command, he merely drove the stallion away.

Now came the fun. For two weeks Bob led the herd. Unlike the stallion, he chose to lead from the front, liking the sound and feel of the wild horses so close behind. He led them to the river and watched happily as they splashed and rolled in the water. Like the stallion, however, he kept his eyes and ears alert for any sign of danger. Sometimes he would pretend he heard something when he hadn't and would lead the herd quickly away simply as a test of their responsiveness to him.

At night he stopped, unsaddled his horse, and laid out his blanket. The herd grazed around him. During all this time he never spoke a word to the horses, not knowing what effect the sound of a voice might have on them. Sometimes he wondered what his own voice sounded like and even wondered if after some period of inactivity, he would return to the ranch and find himself able only to snort and neigh, as these were the only sounds he heard. There were other sounds though, sounds that he couldn't reproduce, like the flaring nostrils of the horses when they were galloping, the dark, bulging eyes, the flesh quivering and shaking. He knew that he couldn't hear any of these things—not with his ears at least. But some-where in his body he heard every ripple of muscles and bending of bones.

The longer he was with the herd, the less he thought. His mind slowly emptied itself of anything relating to his other life and refilled with sky, plain, grass, water, and shrubs. At these times he was more aware of the full-bodied animal beneath him. His own body seemed to take on a new life and he was aware of the wind against his chest, of the taut muscles in his strong legs and the strength of his muscles in his arms, which felt to him like the forelegs of his horses. The only thing he didn't feel he had was a tail to float in the wind behind him.

Finally, when he knew that the herd would follow him anywhere, it was time to take it in. It was a day he tried to keep away as long as possible. But even he began to tire of going back to the west pasture for food and some-times having to chase a horse that had tried to run away from the herd. He had also begun to weary of sleeping under a blanket on the ground every night. So one day, almost a month after he had left, he rode back toward the ranch until he saw one of the cowhands and told him to get the corral ready. Tomorrow he was bringing them in.

The following morning he led the herd on what he imagined was the ride of their lives. Mustangs were made to run. All of his most vivid memories were of mustangs and he remembered the day he had seen a herd of what must have been at least a thousand of them galloping across the plains. The earth was a dark ripple of movement, like the swollen Nueces at floodtime. And though his herd was much smaller, they ran no less beautifully that day.

Then, toward evening, Bob led them east, galloping, galloping, across the plains. And as he led them toward the corral, he knew that no one could ever know these horses by riding on them. One had to ride with them, feeling their hooves pound and shake the earth, their bodies glistening so close by that you could see the thin straight hairs of their shining coats. He led them past the west pasture, down the slope, and just before the corral gate, he swerved to one side, letting the horses thunder inside. The cowboys leaped and shouted, but Bob didn't stay to hear their congratulations. He slowed his mare to a trot and then to a walk to cool her off. It was after dark when he returned to the ranch.

He took his horse to the stable, brushed her down, and put her in a stall for a well-earned meal of hay. Then he walked over to the corral, where the mustangs milled restlessly. He sat on the rail for a long while, looking at them. They were only horses now. Just as he was only a man.

After a while he climbed down from the fence and went into the bunkhouse to go to sleep.

WHEN FREEDOM CAME

BONG!
BONG!
BONG!

The slaves looked up at the sound of the bell. None of them could remember ever hearing the bell in the afternoon. It always woke them in the morning, and the only other time it would ring was after they came from the fields and massa wanted them to come to the big house to see someone get a whipping.

"What you reckon he called us out of the fields for, Jake?" Sarah asked the tall black man next to her.

Jake shook his head. "Don't know. You suppose what we heard about us being free is true? Maybe he's calling us to the big house to tell us we free."

Sarah laughed. "You better get that notion out of your head. If we was free, you don't think he'd ever tell us himself, do you?"

"I suppose not. Well, let's go see what it is. He probably done sold all of us and our new massa is waiting to take us."

"That's more like the truth."

As Jake and Sarah started to leave the field, the other slaves followed slowly. There were only ten of them on the Brower place now. The older ones, like Aunt Kate who worked in the big house, could remember the days when there were more than fifty slaves on the plantation. But that had been a long time ago. And even Jake could remember when there had been a lot more than there were now. A lot of them had been sold, and with the coming of the war some had run away. And those who remained were hoping to get away at the first opportunity.

When they gathered in the yard at the big house, Massa Brower was standing on the porch, his hands gripping the railing tightly. "Well, I guess you must be wondering why I called you out of the fields in the middle of the day." He grinned nervously at the ten expression-

107

less faces below him, faces that were trying to prepare themselves not to feel any emotion when they heard whatever the bad news was. "I don't rightly know how to tell you this. And I guess the only way to say it is just to come out and say it. The South done lost the war. I just heard the news yesterday that General Lee surrendered to the Yankees. So that means that all the slaves is free." He paused a moment, waiting for a reaction, but there was none. "That's right," he repeated. "All the niggers is free now. You can do what you want to. You don't have to work for me no more."

The slaves stood motionless, hearing what he had said and yet being uncertain that there wasn't some trick to it. So no one said anything. They simply waited to hear the rest.

"Well, what you standing there for looking up at me?" Brower said impatiently. "You free! Free as a white man!"

And perhaps it was that "free as a white man" that let them know it was true, because suddenly someone shouted, "Praise God! Praise God!"

"Hallelujah!" someone else yelled and started dancing around in a circle.

"Gonna hoe my own row from now on," came another voice.

Others couldn't say anything, still unable to believe what they had heard.

Brower turned red in the face as he saw the jubilation

on the faces of those who, a minute before, had been his property. He had hoped that they would have thought well enough of him to have shown some regret. After all, he had been a good master. None of them had ever had to worry about a thing. He had taken care of all their needs. When they were sick, he had a doctor come, unlike other slaveowners he knew. He made sure that they'd had new shoes once a year and some meat to eat a couple of times a month. But he guessed he shouldn't expect them to show any gratitude for all he had done for them. They were only niggers. You couldn't expect niggers to be grateful for all the worry and care someone took with them.

"You was right, Jake," Sarah said. "You hear what he say. We free, Jake! We free!"

Jake nodded. "I had a feeling, Sarah. I just had a feeling."

"Ain't you happy? You always look so solemn-like."

He nodded again. "I'm happy, Sarah. Ain't wanted nothing more than to be free since I can remember. I guess since I done thought about it so much, I know that when the rest of 'em stop shouting and carrying on with jubilation, it's suddenly going to hit 'em."

"What's that?"

"Being free ain't easy. It'll hit 'em in the morning when they wake up. Where they gon' get food for breakfast? Where they gon' work at that day? We free, but free don't mean that much if you ain't got a piece of dust in the world to plant a seed in."

"You talk like you think it was better being a slave."

"I ain't saying that, Sarah, and you know it. But you just mind what I say."

The freed slaves went back to their shacks and danced and sang all afternoon. They didn't return to the field but left their hoes lying in the yard at the big house where they had dropped them when they'd heard the news. But that night, when their spirits quieted a little, they began to wonder, What are we supposed to do? No one knew. A couple of the young ones wanted nothing more than to go, and they didn't care where. "I'm just getting away from here," said one. "Maybe I'll go up North. Maybe I won't. But I'm going!"

The older slaves, however, didn't find leaving so easy. "Where am I going to go?" one said bitterly. "Been a slave for fifty years and slaving is all I know."

"You can learn something else, can't you?" one of the young men said.

"Learning ain't easy when you my age."

"Hush up your mouth!" Aunt Kate said sharply. "You ain't old as I is, Jeremiah, and I'm getting away from here so fast in the morning, massa'll think a whirlwind is coming through."

"Where you going?" someone asked.

"Don't make no difference, chile. I'm going. Free means I can come and go as I please and that's something I ain't never been 'lowed to do. I'm going to sleep all day and stay up all night just to see what it feels like." She laughed. "Sho' am. And if a white man tells me to squat, I'm gon' stand. If he say run, I'm gon' walk. If he say jump, I'm gon' roll. Whatever a white man tell me to do, I'm gon' do just the other. Free means I'm gon' do what I want to do when I want to do it and how I want to do it!"

"Talk it, Aunt Kate!" one of the young men said.

"Yes, son. I'm free now and I dare any white man to say a word to me. I just might spit in his face."

Everybody laughed.

When the laughter died, Jeremiah said, "But what you gon' do for food, Aunt Kate? How you gon' eat? Where you gon' work at?"

"Just hush your mouth. That's what's wrong with niggers. They want to know what's gon' happen before they get out of bed in the morning. Listen, Jeremiah. If the Lawd could take care of the Israelites for forty years in the wilderness, He can sho' put a little bacon rind and greens in front of Aunt Kate every once in a while. Now ain't that so?"

"That's right!" a voice assented.

"I ain't worrying about what I'm gon' eat. The Lord'll make a way. I know He will."

Jeremiah wasn't convinced, but Aunt Kate's speech had stopped the worries of the others, and all of them agreed that the next morning they would leave.

"And I tell you something else I'm gon' do," Aunt Kate continued. "I'm gon' change my name."

"How come?"

"I'm free, ain't I?" she responded indignantly. "I can be anybody I want to now. Ain't never had a name of my own. Every time I was sold, my new massa come giving me his name. I'm gon' name myself now. Sho' 'nuf. And you better change yo' name, 'cause you know these white folks. They might decide next week that us niggers should be slaves again. And Massa Brower'll come looking for us. He'll be going through the countryside asking folks if they heard of Kate Brower. Well, the way I figure it is if I'm Kate Williams or Kate Jones, then he won't never find me. I just might change my name every week for a while, 'til I'm sure these white folks ain't gon' bring slavery back."

Nobody could sleep that night. Even though they were tired, they didn't want to sleep away their first night of freedom. And why go to bed if you didn't have to? Jake stayed apart from the celebrating. He sat on the steps of his cabin and watched and listened but said nothing. Finally Sarah came over and sat down beside him.

Sarah was much younger than Jake. She didn't know exactly how old she was, having been sold from her mother when she was still a baby. But Aunt Kate said that she wasn't more than five when she came to the Brower place. If that was true, she was about twenty-five now. She had been purchased to be the servant of Mary Lou, Master Brower's daughter, but Mary Lou had died of typhoid fever a little more than a year after Sarah had come. There was no work in the house for her after that, so she was put to work in the fields. She guessed she had fallen in love with Jake the first time she had seen him. He was much older than she, married, with several children. But even as a little girl she had known that she felt something special for him. She was more than happy to work in the fields, where she could see Jake's strong back glistening with sweat in the hot sun. He scarcely noticed her, though. Not until his wife and children were sold. That was six or seven years ago. She hadn't known what to do for Jake, particularly since she was the same age as his oldest child and that was how he thought of her. She hoped that her constant presence beside him made him feel better. He never said. But she always told herself that neither had he ever told her to go away. Now that they were free, she hoped that Jake would finally see that she was a woman, a woman who would be good to him.

"Anything the matter, Jake?"

"Just thinking."

She looked at him, wanting to reach out and hold him in her arms, but Jake looked closed up inside himself. It always made her sad to see him like that, as if he were locked up in a jail and no one could find the key. Many times she had asked him what he was thinking when he looked that way, but he'd never told her.

Jake *was* glad that Sarah was there. It seemed that ever since Mandy and the children had been sold, Sarah was there. At first he had been annoyed. Surely that young girl didn't think she was going to replace Mandy. But Sarah never acted as if she could. It was obvious, even to him, that she didn't have eyes for anyone on the place except him and would've married him if he had said the word. But she didn't try. After a while Jake understood that she was leaving the choice up to him. She was there and whenever he asked, she would say yes. Jake, however, couldn't see himself marrying a girl the same age as one of his children. Too, she could never have been the help and companion Mandy had been. He'd never known another woman and not a day had passed in the last seven years when he hadn't felt the pain he'd felt that day the overseer came over to Mandy and the children in the field and said that Massa Brower wanted them at the big house on the double. He started to go with them, but the overseer had pushed him back. "Didn't nobody call your name." Just as he had known today that Massa Brower was going to tell them they were free, he had known that day, as they left the field, that he would never see them again. Massa Brower had been selling niggers all spring. He must've been in some kind of money trouble, Jake figured, because he sold almost twenty that year. All that spring he and Mandy had talked about what they would do if they were separated. And all he could say was, "Someday I'd find you. That's all. I'd run away and come to you, Mandy."

He remembered waiting in the fields, waiting as he went down the rows with his hoe, waiting to see them out of the corner of his eye walking back. But they didn't. At sundown, as he left the fields, he hoped that maybe they were at the cabin waiting for him. He knew they couldn't be. No slaves were allowed at their cabins during the day unless they were sick. But he hoped. No one said a word to him as they left the fields, their hoes across their shoulders. He felt someone walking beside him, like a puppy. It was Sarah. But he paid her no attention, being unable to feel anything except a hurting like he had never known before. He walked down the slave row, and it was quiet, like a cemetery. He kept trying to see someone running out of his cabin or hear some noise inside, but there was nothing. When he walked inside, the pallets where they had slept the night before were gone. He looked all around the room and there wasn't even a thread to indicate that Mandy and the children had lived there. It was as if they had never existed.

His face took on the solemn look that made Sarah nervous that day. Everybody did what they could for him. During the next few days, every slave on the place came up to him and expressed their sorrow. He thanked each one, but their concern didn't help. Nothing would ever help, not even finding Mandy one day. Being with her again wouldn't erase that pain of standing helpless while another man took his family away from him. No man would let another man sell his wife, except a nigger. Yet he knew that all he could've done was to try and kill massa and gotten killed himself. And what would that have accomplished? Massa still would have sold them. Yet sometimes he thought it would have been better to have done something. Instead he'd just continued hoeing.

A week or so afterward he'd run away to look for them. But he hadn't gotten far before he was caught, brought back, and whipped. After that he hadn't tried again. Now, however, he was free, and before he could do anything else, he had to find Mandy. After that he would worry about what to do with his freedom.

He looked at Sarah, wondering how he could tell her. He didn't want to hurt her, but he hadn't encouraged her to love him. But he guessed he hadn't discouraged her either. Maybe if Mandy had died, he could think about marrying such a young girl. But as long as Mandy was someplace in the world, he couldn't look at another woman. He just knew that somewhere Mandy was free now, too, and she would be standing by the road looking for him.

"Jake?" Sarah said softly, breaking the silence.

116

"Hm?"

"What you gon' do now that we free? You gon' leave like everybody else?"

"I reckon I will."

"Where you going?"

"To look for Mandy." He said it as gently as he knew how.

Now that he had said it, Sarah noticed that she really wasn't surprised. In fact she had been expecting him to say that. "And what if you can't find her?"

"I'll find her. I'll keep looking till the day I die."

"But what if you find her and she done married another man?"

"You'd better watch your mouth, girl!" Jake said angrily.

"I didn't mean nothing," she said hastily.

"You just saying that to get me to marry you. You been after me ever since they took Mandy away. You just hoping she's dead or married to somebody else. If she's living, Mandy's waiting for me, just like I been waiting for her all these years. And I don't want to hear you saying nothing about it. You hear me?"

She had never seen him angry and it frightened her. "Jake, please, I didn't mean nothing by it. I was just thinking about you, not wanting you to be hurt. That's all."

"What you know about hurt? A young girl like you.

117

Nothing but a child. You don't know what hurt is, Sarah."

"If hurt is loving a man who don't love you, maybe I know a little of what it's about."

Jake nodded slowly. "I'm sorry, Sarah. I had no business saying all them things. I guess you just hit a sore spot, that's all. It done occurred to me that Mandy might be married to another man. But I can't believe that. I just can't, Sarah. I told her that if we was ever separated, I'd find her. And she said she'd wait."

"Well, for your sake, I hope she did. I hope she did, Jake."

Daybreak found the slave quarter alive with activity. Everyone, including the frightened Jeremiah, was packing his few belongings and preparing to go. Sarah was sitting on the steps of her and Aunt Kate's cabin waiting for Jake to come out. When he did, she walked over to him. He smiled when he saw her. "Sarah, I'm sorry for all them things I said last night. And I just want you to know that I wasn't unmindful of you. It was just nice knowing you was there all the time, walking by my side. I guess it wasn't easy for you, and I would've been more mindful of you if my mind hadn't been somewheres else."

"I know, Jake."

"But you too pretty a girl to be waiting on an old man like me. There's a lot of young boys around here will make you a good husband."

"You mind your business, Jake. Don't be telling me how to run my life."

Jake chuckled. "Okay. Where you going?"

She shrugged. "Don't know. Aunt Kate say she going and don't much care where. So I'll just go along with her. I expect this time next week she'll be tired of going and we'll settle somewhere. White folks are still gon' need somebody to cook their food for 'em and Aunt Kate can't do nothing else. And I don't reckon white folks going to be ready to get out in them fields and work to make a crop either. So we'll stop when Aunt Kate gets tired, and she'll go back to the kitchen and I'll go back to the fields. We don't know nothing else, do we, even if we is free?"

He nodded. "Well, maybe you'll learn something else. Maybe now you can go to a school and get some learning."

"Maybe."

"Well, Sarah. I'm off."

"Good luck to you, Jake."

"Thank you, Sarah. Thank you."

He knew Sarah was watching him as he walked up the slave row to the big house, but he didn't look back. He was leaving and when you left a place, you only looked to where you were going. And all he could see was Mandy standing by a road somewhere, looking for him.

He walked past the barn, the pig trough, and the well into the backyard of the big house. Stepping on the back

119

porch, he knocked on the door. After a moment Massa Brower opened it. "Morning, Jake. You leaving me, I guess."

"Yessuh. I just want to know where you sold my family to."

"Oh. I been meaning to tell you how sorry I was about that, Jake."

"Yessuh."

"Owning niggers wasn't easy, you know. And I, for one, am glad it's all over with."

"Yessuh."

"I didn't want to sell Mandy. She was a good nigger. Hard worker."

"Yessuh."

"But I had to. You understand, don't you? I was in a whole lot of debt and had to raise some cash in a hurry."

"Yessuh."

"If it hadn't been for that, nothing on earth could've made me sell her."

"Yessuh. I just wants to know where you sold them to."

"They probably ain't there no more, Jake. What with the war and all. Ain't nobody where they was. Everything's turned upside down and every kind of way."

"Yessuh. I reckon the best place to start looking is the last place they was at."

Brower nodded. "Well, a man named Allen bought

'em. William Allen. From Pulaski, Tennessee, he said he was."

"Yessuh. Which way is that?"

"Well, it's east, but, Jake, that's a long ways off."

"Yessuh." And Jake walked away.

Pulaski, Tennessee, was more than five hundred miles from Pine Bluff, Arkansas. Jake wished he was a bird and could have flown those miles in a couple of days. But he had to walk them, one step at a time, one foot in front of the other. And he couldn't walk every day, because he had to stop and work to get at least enough to eat. Sometimes he got paid in money, and for a few days he could travel and buy enough to eat.

There were a lot of ex-slaves traveling the roads. Some were also looking for children, wives, husbands, or parents who had been sold. It helped him to know that he wasn't the only one. Some he talked to hadn't seen their mothers since they were children. He knew how they felt. It helped a man to know where he was from if he knew where his mother was. His mother lay in the slave burying ground on the plantation.

He wondered sometimes how many people looking for loved ones would find them, including himself. In a way it was a foolish thing to do. But there was no way not to do it. Every day someone asked him if he knew such-and-such a person or if he had heard anything about them.

After three months on the road he found that he had a vast store of information and several times was able to direct someone a little closer to the person he was looking for. And just as he was asked, he asked. But it wasn't until he had passed through Nashville, Tennessee, did he find someone who thought she knew Mandy. It was an old woman, who reminded him of Aunt Kate, walking down the road with a bundle on her head. Like many others, she didn't know where she was going but, "Where ain't as important as the going, son," she said, laughing. "You know when you let a chicken out of a coop, it don't have the slightest idea where it's going. Might run out in the woods and get eaten by a fox first thing. But all the chickens know is to get away from the coop."

He asked her about Mandy and gave a description of her.

The old lady nodded. "She got some children?"

Jake nodded.

"And she dark skin, you say? Like you is?"

"That's right," he said, getting excited.

"Well, if it's the same Mandy, she live on Mr. Jim Jenkenson's place on the other side of Pulaski. When you gets in the vicinity, son, you just ask somebody to direct you to Mr. Jim Jenkenson's place. Everybody 'round there know where it is. If it's the same Mandy, she be out there."

"How many days walking is that?"

"Three days if you stroll. Two and a half if you walk fast. And a day if you can hitch a ride on somebody's mule cart."

Jake tried not to let himself get too excited. It might be another Mandy. It was a common name. But the old woman said it was outside of Pulaski and that was where Mandy had been sold, too. Still, he kept his feelings inside of him, as if they were a present tied up in a red ribbon which he could open only on Christmas.

It took him two days of fast walking with little sleep to get to Pulaski, and the first person he asked directed him to continue down the road for another two miles. He asked that person if he knew Mandy, and the person nodded and said Mandy had six children. Jake was disappointed. Mandy only had four. He almost didn't go any farther, but since he was so close, he decided to go on. Maybe the person had made a mistake about the number of children she had.

She was walking down the road carrying a bucket of water on her head when he saw her. He knew it was she, the one arm raised over her head, resting lightly against the bucket, the other arm swinging loosely at her side. He had always loved the easy way Mandy had of walking, even with a bucket of water on her head. She never looked like she was working. He started to call out her name, but stopped. It was just possible that it was somebody else.

123

Sometimes every woman he saw looked like Mandy, so he started running to catch up with her.

The woman heard the hurried steps behind her and stopped to look back. Jake saw the soft black face he had loved all of his life and shouted, "It's you! It's you! Mandy!" He ran up to her, tears running down his face. "Oh, thank God. Mandy!"

"Jake? Is that you, Jake?"

"It ain't Abraham Lincoln," he said, laughing.

She gazed at him, uncertain what to do. Then, letting her hand drop from the bucket she screamed, "Jake!" as the bucket tumbled from her head and water splashed both of them. She flung her arms around him, laughing. "Jake, Jake, Jake. It is you, ain't it?"

And with the feel of her arms pressing against his back, Jake felt himself come to life for the first time since he'd last seen her. He buried his face in her neck. "I told you that if anything ever happened, I'd find you. I told you, didn't I?"

"You look just the same," Mandy said, looking at him. "Just the same." She stepped out of his arms and picked up the bucket, laughing. "Look what you made me do. Now I got to go all the way back to the spring and get some more."

"Well, come on. How's Charles and Mary Ann and Caesar and Carl?" he asked, referring to the children.

"Oh, they fine. You probably won't recognize none of 'em. They so big now."

He laughed. "And to think that I almost didn't come out here."

"What you mean?"

"Well, I asked after you in town and a man said he knew of a Mandy who had six children and since we only got four, I just figured it was another Mandy. I almost didn't come, till it occurred to me that he might have made a mistake."

They came to the spring and Mandy bent to fill the bucket.

"Let me do it," Jake said. "You ain't gon' be toting no more water now. And anyway, how come Charles or one of the other children didn't come and get it?"

"They out in the field."

"Well, from now on you ain't gon' be doing no more of that heavy lifting and work like that." Jake filled the bucket. "I never could carry it on my head like you."

"Jake? Set that bucket down." She laughed, looking at him trying to set it on his head.

"I'll carry it," Jake said proudly.

"Set it down," she said, suddenly sad.

He put it on the ground and looked at her. "Anything the matter?"

She nodded. "I ain't your wife no more, Jake," she said

sadly, looking at her feet. "That man in town what told you I got six children now was telling the truth. I should've told you back on the road when you brought it up. But I didn't know how to tell you."

"You ain't married to somebody else?"

She nodded and broke into tears. "How was I to know for sure you'd find me, Jake? I could've waited for you until the day I died and you never showed up 'cause you was dead or had done married somebody else."

"Aw, Mandy," he cried, taking her in his arms. "But I told you I'd find you, didn't I? I told you that!"

"I know, Jake, and I wanted to believe you. God knows I did. But a woman gets lonesome, Jake. And Henry was a nice man. The children liked him, too. So we jumped the broom and I prayed that this time the Lord wouldn't let me or him be sold away from each other. And after we was freed, the first thing we done was to go and get married like white folks do, and get a piece of paper so couldn't nobody come and separate us. If I'd known, Jake, I wouldn't have done it. But a woman gets lonesome."

"So do a man," he sobbed. "So do a man."

They held each other tightly for a while. "I just wish I'd known, Jake," she whispered softly, stepping back and wiping her eyes.

"Mandy? You ain't got to stay, do you?" Jake said, getting excited. "Now that I'm here, you can leave and come with me."

126

Mandy shook her head. "I can't do that, Jake. I swore before God and the preacher to be with Henry until one of us died. And, plus, we got married by the paper, the way the white folks do. And when you get the paper, you married sho' 'nuf. It ain't like jumping the broom. Like we done in slavery time. We ain't slaves no more, Jake. We got to live by the paper now."

"But, Mandy, I love you! I ain't thought about nothing else for seven years but you!"

She started crying again. "I loves you, too, Jake. God knows I do. But Henry's a good man, and I don't love him like I do you, but I guess I love him. I loved him enough to get married by the paper."

Jake shook his head repeatedly, muttering, "No, no, no, no. It ain't right. First they come and take you away, sell you like you a bale of cotton. They don't ask me how my heart feels about it. Just sell you away. Then you meets somebody you don't love like you love me, but they give you a piece of paper saying you got to be with him, though you love me. It ain't right, Mandy. It just ain't right."

"But that's the way it is, Jake. Wasn't right for us to be slaves all them years neither, but that was the way it was." She picked up the bucket of water and hoisted it to her head. "I—I got to be getting back, Jake. You want to come see the children? I know Henry wouldn't mind. I told him all about you and he say you sound like a very good man, the kind of man he'd like to know. I know

127

you'd like him, too, Jake. Ain't none of this his fault."

"I know that, Mandy. But I reckon not. I don't think I could stand seeing another man happy with you."

She nodded. "I understands."

She started up the path from the spring to the road. Jake didn't move. He raised his head and watched the easy swaying of her body. When she got to the road she turned and looked at him. He could see the tears coming down her face.

"I wish I'd known, Jake."

"God knows, I wished you had too, Mandy," he said, biting his lip and sobbing as he watched her walk down the road and out of sight.

LONG JOURNEY HOME

I definitely do remember slavery days, son. Of course, I don't remember 'em for myself. I was just a little thing when the Surrender came, but my mama and my grand-mama, they told me all about the slavery days. So I re-members it for them. And back there when I was coming up after the Surrender, well, it was so close to slavery days that I could smell 'em real good, even if I didn't go through for myself.

Lawd, chile, them was terrible days. Terrible days.

Don't let nobody tell you no different. You hear? I don't care what they tells you in school. They may be teaching you right, but if you sitting here asking me about them days, well, they must not be doing too good a job over there at that schoolhouse. When I was coming up, wasn't too many of us knew nothing about no school. Back in them days wasn't too many whites went to school, either. We just all growed up ignorant together. But to tell the God's truth, don't seem much different today, and now everybody's going to school.

But that ain't what you asked me about. You say you wants to hear about slavery time. Well, from the way I hear my mama and grandmama tell it, slavery was work. That's all it was from the time you could walk till they tied your carcass on a flat piece of board and put you in the ground. Grandmama used to say that her ol' miss had her doing little things when she was three and by the time she was seven, she was putting in a day's work in the field just like the grownups was. That's the truth. Wasn't no *child*hood back in them days. None in mine either, for that matter. Ain't never heard of such. I guess Grandmama played a few games like you children do now, but that's *all* you all do. Back in them days the overseer would give a child a task of cotton to pick just like he give one to a grownup. And if that child didn't pick his task every day, he got a whipping just like anybody else.

Mama say the worst times was at the time of the full

131

moon. The full moon be so bright, her ol' massa would make 'em work in the night too. She say them cotton bolls would shine so bright in the moonlight too. She used to wonder how come the Lawd didn't make cotton black so it couldn't be seen so good in the moonlight. She just couldn't understand that.

You young folks don't know nothing about no hard times. Oh, I know y'all ain't got it easy, but at least you can go where you wants to and when you wants to. Back in slavery time, a colored man had to have a pass. Sho' did. Had to get permission to go off the plantation, and any white man who saw him could stop him and ask to see his pass. And shame on him if he didn't have one. My mama say once her ol' miss sent her into town to buy some things, and a little white boy about ten years old stopped her and asked to see her pass. And she was a grown woman. But she had to stand there while this child, that's right, a *child*, looked at her pass and then gave her permission to go on. Mama say she was scared to death that that boy was going to tear the pass up and then say she didn't have one and take her in to the high sheriff. That used to happen too. Some of them mean-minded white people who didn't have nothing to do but make trouble for colored people would take their passes and tear 'em up and then turn 'em in to the sheriff, who would beat 'em for being runaways. And then when their massa finally came to get 'em, they couldn't say that a white man had taken their pass and tore it up. They had to say they lost it, and then massa would give 'em another beating.

What you ask me, son? How come my mama didn't run away? How come she didn't fight back? Well, what makes you think she didn't want to? When you knew her, she was old. Didn't want to do nothing but sit here on the porch and smoke her pipe and watch the folks go down the road. She probably didn't look like much of a woman then, but, son, let me tell you. That woman worked like a man all her life. I done seen her get up befo' breakfast and chop a load of kindling wood and then go out in the field and clear new ground all day, come home and cook, carry in water for the next morning and then do some mending before she went to bed. That ol' woman was strong and if she had had half a chance, wouldn't have been no slavery that could've held her down. That's the God's truth.

You think 'cause she never run away or kill nobody trying that she must've liked slavery. That's what you think, don't you? Well, son, when you get grown you just might learn that there might be something you hate with everything in you, but ain't a thing you can do about it. And that's the way slavery was. Just because they didn't get away from it don't mean they was happy. Like I said, you didn't know your grandmama too much, but let me tell you. That ol' woman didn't speak to a white person after the Surrender. That's true! She hated 'em worse than you youngsters do now. That's how come we living in a town where there ain't nothing but colored people. After the Surrender there was some, like Mama, who said that if they lived to be a thousand years old and never saw another white person, it would be too soon. So what they done was they worked for white people for a few years and saved their money. And then they left and come down here in Florida until they found some land that nobody wanted, land that was cheap, and they bought it and set up this town. It turned out that that land wasn't as bad as white folks thought it was, plus they could make a living fishing, you know, so it was all right. And so far as I know, your grandmama didn't speak to a white person from the day we moved into this house until the day she died. Over thirty-five years.

But you see, back in slavery time, it was hard to fight. I done seen you grab a snake behind his head, and as long as you hold him like that, all he can do is wiggle. But he can't bite. Well, that's the way it was in slavery time. The white folks had that thing fixed so all colored people could do was wiggle, and they bet not wiggle too much either. The white folks knew that if somebody had been holding them slaves, they would have risen up first chance they got. So they just made sure that them slaves never had that first chance. Why, they would slap you if you looked a white man in the eye. That's the truth! You was supposed to keep your eyes on the ground when talking to a white man. And even when I was coming up after the Surrender, why I heard tell of colored people what got lynched 'cause they didn't get off the sidewalk when they saw a white woman coming.

Don't you be looking at me like you think I'm touched in the head, boy! I know what I'm talking about. I'm telling you what I know, not what I think. You hear me? If all this sounds a little crazy, it ain't me what's crazy. It's them white people. And there's some mean ones, son. You don't know too much about 'em, growing up here like you doing. But there's some mean ones out there. In the Bible, I understand, it say the Devil is red and he got a long tail and pointed ears. Naw, son. I don't mean to be disputing with the Lawd, but He got it wrong this time. The Devil is white and he looks just like a cracker. Only thing red about him is his neck.

Mama say that back in slavery time they used to go way back out in the woods at night and pray for deliverance. Pray and ask the Lawd to please send Moses back to lead 'em out of bondage, to send down a plague like he done on them Egyptians back then, to make the blood run through the furrows in the field as a warning to the white folks to change their ways and let the slaves go. Mama say back in them days they sho' 'nuf did some praying and singing. That praying you hear Reverend Solomon do now, it's all right. He can put down a good prayer, but

135

wasn't nothing like them ol' slavery-time folks praying. 'Cause they had good reason to pray. The Lawd finally did deliver 'em from their bondage, but seem to me He sho' took His time about doing it. That's how come I don't go to church too much now. Any Lawd that slow about relieving people's suffering ain't too good at His job, you ask me. I want me a right-now God! The white folks taught us all about a God who would take care of things in the sweet bye-'n-bye. Well, that don't do much good if today is sour as a pickle when you got the mumps. Now ain't that the truth?

Don't you go 'round here thinking that they liked slavery. They did what they could. You have to understand, though, that they didn't have much to fight with. Where was they gon' get some guns from? And even if they did get some, the white folks always had more. And it's hard to run away from slavery if all you know is a place called the Nawth. You don't know nothing about it, but you just heard that colored people wasn't slaves up there. For a lot of slaves that was enough. Off they went. But to go from Georgia, where Mama was, to the Nawth is a whole lot of stepping. You hear me? Some of 'em walked it. Sho' did. But for all them that tried, I don't reckon too many made it. Most of 'em got caught.

So them that stayed behind did what wiggling they could. Mama say she used to be the cook, but even back then she hated white folks. Some of the slavery people

136

didn't, you know. They was proud to work around white folks. Thought maybe they'd turn white if they got close enough. Not her! She say she used to spit in all the food before she served it. And she say it wasn't no little bit either. Say she would work all day getting a whole mouthful and then spit it in the stew or whatever it was, stir it up real good, and put it on the table. Ha! Ha! Ha! Chile, don't you know she would almost fall over laughing when ol' massa would tell her what a good dinner it was. Yes, son, that was one mean ol' lady when she wanted to be. One time she tell me about grinding up glass real fine till it was like a powder. Say she'd stay up all night, practically, hiding out in the woods so not even none of the niggers knew what she was doing. She sit out there and break this glass, then chip it up into little pieces, then grind it real fine, put it in a little bag that the white folks thought she carried her snuff in. She'd dump that glass in the stew or one of them thick soups, stir it up, and put it on the table. Ha! Ha! They finally sent her to work in the fields, 'cause one day she set the kitchen on fire. They didn't know that. They thought it was an accident, but it wasn't no accident. Back in them times the kitchen wasn't in the house like it is now. It was a separate little house back of the big house. There be a big ol' stove, and a oven and a whole heap of kindling wood, and Mama say that on them hot summer days she would've rather been shoveling coal into Hell's furnaces than be in that kitchen, 'cause the Devil wouldn't have made Hell that hot. She say she'd keep a big pitcher of water right outside the kitchen in the shade and drink two, three gallons a day. 'Cause that heat was just drawing all the water out of her body and she had to keep putting more water in. Well, one day, she said, ol' miss wanted her to fix breakfast, then bake a whole bunch of pies and cakes, and after that make supper. The pies and cakes was for some party ol' miss was planning. Mama say she went straight out to the kitchen and started putting kindling wood in the stove and put in more and more, and then she took a tiny bit of kerosene. Don't take much you know. And put that little bit of kerosene on that fire and there she blow. She say that they was some mad white folks, too, 'cause she hadn't even fixed breakfast. And you know how evil folks can get when they hungry. She got a whipping for it. Sho' did. Carried the scars from that whipping right on into her grave with her. But she say it was worth it. Say that fire even burned part of the big house.

So they sent her to the field. 'Course wasn't nothing they could give her to do but she wasn't going to try to mess up. Not so long as she was a slave, that is. She didn't like working in the field any more than she'd liked being the cook and the ol' overseer didn't like her attitude. You see, son, your attitude was a big thing back then. 'Cause them white folks not only wanted you to be they slave, they wanted you to enjoy it. That's the truth! So you was supposed to grin and bow your head and look like you was having a good time. If you did that, you was a good nigger. Well, my mama couldn't do that. Not on your life. If she didn't like something, it showed all over her face. She couldn't hide what she was feeling most of the time. So they said she had a bad attitude. Well, one day the overseer came over to where she was in the field and pulled back his whip and let her have it one time. Mama had swore after she got that beating for the fire that she'd die before she let another white man put the whip to her. She turned around and before that po' cracker knew what was happening, she had grabbed that whip and *Crack!* Mama say she tore his shirt off his back with it. And massa was scared to do a thing to her about it too. So he got rid of her. Sold her. He had to get rid of her, 'cause if the other slaves saw Mama beating up the overseer, well, they might get it into their head that they could do the same thing. And massa didn't want 'em getting no notions like that. Not that anybody had to teach 'em. Can't no colored person teach another colored person to hate white folks. White folks do it they ownself.

There was women back in them times what would kill their own children rather than see them brought up as slaves. Baby would be born and the mother would just smother that po' little thing with a piece of cloth. I praise

139

the Lawd my mama didn't hate slavery that much. But there was them that did. Some folks would even kill themselves.

Your great-grandmama was a pure-blooded African. That's right. And I reckon it was all that African blood in your grandmama what made her so mean. Your great-grandmama was brought over here from Africa when she was a little bitty girl. She was a small, dried-up black woman. Didn't nobody know how old she was when she died, but she had to be over a hundred. Looked like she was old as dirt.

She was smart! Let me tell you, son. She couldn't read or write, but she could read them trees and bushes out there. Sho' could. Wish I knew all she knew. She would go through the woods every spring and pick a leaf off this and dig up the root of that and pull some bark from something else, and then she'd grind this, and boil the other, and do who knows what-all and she was better than them white doctors and didn't charge nothing. Well, the white folks brought her over here on a ship. She say she was just a little girl then and lived in this village someplace in Africa. She never was able to tell me whereabouts in Africa, not that I would've knowed if she had told me. But she said she could find it if she went there.

Anyway, she say one night some people from another tribe came swooping down on her village and before anybody knew what was happening, they'd caught and tied

140

up everyone there. Didn't nobody know what was happening, since her people spoke a different tongue from the ones what caught 'em. What I gather from her was that they don't speak English in Africa, but all different kinds of languages. She say the name of her people was Hibos, or Ibos, or something like that. Anyway, she say they marched for many days until they started hearing this great roaring noise. Say it was the loudest thing she ever heard in her life. It sounded like thunder, but it never stopped, and the more they walked, the louder the noise got.

They was scared, not knowing where they was going or what was happening or nothing. Well, one day they suddenly came out of the forest and there, right in front of them, was what was making the noise. You know what it was? It was the ocean. She say she never seen no water like that before. Water what rise up big and hit the land over and over, never stopping. And so much water. She say she didn't know there was so much water. It was a terrible sight, she said.

Well, the ones what caught her and her people put 'em in a big pen close by the ocean and kept them there for two or three moons. She said she remember it was night of the full moon when they arrived there and her daddy counted two more full moons before they were finally put on the ships. It was one night after the third moon had passed that they was tied up again and led down to the beach. They was put in boats and rowed out to this big ship. She say it was black people what rowed 'em out to the ship, but once they was put on board, she saw the ugliest people she'd ever seen in her life. Scared her plumb to death! Folks didn't have no color on 'em at all. She said she had to look real hard to find their mouth and their nose. And their hair was the color of camel dung. She say she clung real close to her mother. Them people just didn't look right.

The white people put 'em all in the bottom of the ship, where they made 'em lie down. Say it wasn't no higher than the space underneath the porch where you crawl at to play. Couldn't nobody stand up down there. They had to lay on their back and then they were all chained together some kind of way. To her dying day I don't think she ever got over that. She was old as water when I knew her and I remember some nights she would be lying in her sleep, twisting and turning and talking about how hot it was and how much it smelled. She was dreaming that she was back on that slave boat. That's what it was. She didn't like to talk about it, but once she did. It was awful, son! Just awful! Wasn't no windows down there, so the air couldn't circulate. And the people had to go to the toilet just lying where they was. They couldn't get up. So they had to lie there in they own mess and everybody else's mess and after a couple of days, you can imagine what it smelled like down there. I can't think of nothing more terrible! She say once in a while they would unchain 'em and take everybody up on the deck of the ship so they could get some air and walk around a little and some of the white men would clean up all the mess and air the place out a little. But she said they only did that twice and then they stopped 'cause every time they did it, a whole bunch of folks would walk up onto the deck and before anybody could stop 'em, they'd jump overboard. That's right! Jump right on over the side of the ship and into the ocean and drown or the sharks would eat 'em. Say some of the folks thought it was better to die than go through something like that. Some of the women would grab their little children and jump over with their children.

Her folks died on the ship of some disease. Of course, with folks having to lie in they own mess, it's a wonder to me that all of 'em didn't die. I know I would have. She say a whole lot of folks died and the white men would come down and drag them up on the deck and throw 'em over like they was a sack of rotten potatoes. Didn't even take the time to say a few words over their body. Just pitch 'em over.

Well, finally they got here. Landed at some place in Georgia. 'Course them Africans didn't have the slightest idea where they was. They'd never heard of America, never seen no white folks, but she say she knew she was a long way from home when she saw how many white folks there was. And the black people spoke the same

143

tongue as the white people. She and her people, though, still talked in their own tongue. They started to pick up English, but you know she always spoke it kinna funny. She didn't talk African no more 'cause wasn't nobody around to talk it with, but every now and then, I'd hear her singing something that didn't make no kind of sense at all. That was when she'd be singing in African.

Well, she said that they took 'em to a plantation right near the ocean. Guess it was a rice plantation. Them the only ones near the ocean I know of. They learned how to do the work and they started in slaving from sunup to sundown. They caught on pretty quick that they was slaves. Don't know what the word for it is in African, but must be one 'cause she said they knew they was slaves. And they wasn't too happy about it. They were homesick, not to mention sick about being slaves. I try to think sometimes what it must've been like for her. She used to sit here on the porch and talk to me like I'm talking to you. Pipe in her mouth. Rag tied around her head. And I'd look up at her and she'd be staring way off somewhere and I wished I could be inside her head to see what she was seeing. She wouldn't be seeing that vegetable patch over there. Or them woods behind it. She was seeing Africa just as clear as you seeing me right now. And I wished I could feel what she was feeling. It must've been a painful thing for them Africans what first come here. Taken away from they home like that. Being sailed across the ocean and pushed

144

off the boat at a place they'd never heard of. That's enough reason for hating white folks right there. They just took her life and did with it what *they* wanted to. Didn't ask her what she thought about. Just went on and took her life and changed it all around. She was only a little girl, but 'cause she was little don't mean she didn't feel it. I know she felt it, the way she used to scream and holler in her sleep.

She say it wasn't working the fields that was bad. They had fields in Africa and all the women worked 'em every day. But it was their own fields. That was the difference. And they could talk and sing while they worked and have a good time. But the white folks didn't like for her and her people to be talking African to each other. See, white folks didn't know no African. So they could've been talking about how they was going to get away and the white folks wouldn't have known a thing about it. White folks made 'em talk English. But she say at night, when the white folks wasn't around, they'd talk African and talk about how unhappy they was and how much they missed they home.

Well, one night they was talking and they decided they was going home. Decided that they wasn't going to slave no more. They was going home. So the next morning bright and early they got up. Long before the white folks was up they was up and they started walking. And they walked until they heard the roaring water. And they kept walking. And the roaring got louder and louder as they got closer. And they didn't look back. Not once. They just marched on down to the beach, and without slowing down one bit, walked right on into the ocean. Just walked in, one by one, and kept walking until the water cover 'em up. Must've been forty or fifty of 'em. Grandmama say she was there, but she got scared. Say the water was so loud and it was churning and foaming up and she just got scared. So she was left standing on the beach till somebody seen her and took her back to the plantation.

Them ol' ignorant slaves whose family had been away from Africa so long that they couldn't remember nothing in their bones, well, they say them Africans drowned themselves. But she say wasn't so. She say the gods took care of 'em. See, in Africa they got more than one god. They got a whole bunch of 'em. That make more sense to me. Never did see how no one god could handle all the problems in the world. In Africa they got gods take care of anything and everything—fire, wind, water, love— you name it. Just like over here if you want a house built, you don't ask the car mechanic. You ask the carpenter. Well, that's how it is with the gods. These white folks talk about praying to one god. Shoot! Ain't no way he gon' handle all the things got to be handled. So them Africans didn't drown, honey. Don't you believe it. Whatever god was in charge of that took care of 'em. And since they didn't have no boat, they just walked back to

146

Africa and went on back to their village, and you and me got cousins and aunts and uncles and half-brothers and sisters sitting up in Africa right now that we don't know a thing about. But I bet if we could find the village where Grandmama was from and we told 'em that story, they'd know us.

Sometimes I wish I knew what god it was them Africans talked to. You ask one of them teachers over there at the school to look up in one of them books what god it was. And what you say to him. 'Cause, chile, I'd be off this porch and walking home in a minute. Ain't nothing here for us black folks but bad luck and trouble.

Notes

"Satan on My Track" is based on interviews with and readings about rural blues singers—Bukka White, Son House, Robert Johnson, Muddy Waters, and Charlie Patton.

"Louis" is based on a true story recounted in the *Reminiscences of Levi Coffin*. Coffin was considered the "president" of the Underground Railroad.

"Ben" is based on a true story that can be found in *Colored Patriots of the American Revolution* by William C. Nell.

Bob Lemmons is mentioned in two books: *The Adventures of the Negro Cowboys* by Philip Durham and *The Mustangs* by Everett L. Jones and J. Frank Dobie. In the latter there is a short interview with Lemmons done in the late thirties by Dobie when Lemmons was in his eighties.

"When Freedom Came" recounts an occurrence common during the early years following Emancipation.

"Long Journey Home" was inspired by a footnote in *Drums and Shadows* (published by the Federal Writers' Project), which was a study of African survivals in coastal Georgia. The footnote refers to a place in Georgia called Ybo Landing, where, it is reported, a number of Ibos walked into the sea. Exactly where Ybo Landing is I don't know, as it was not on any maps of Georgia I examined. It is, perhaps, a local name.

About the Author

Julius Lester is the critically acclaimed author of books for both young people and adults. In addition to *Long Journey Home: Stories from Black History* his books for Dial include *To Be a Slave*, a Newbery Honor Book; *This Strange New Feeling*, a Coretta Scott King Honor Book; and *The Knee-High Man and Other Tales*, an ALA Notable Book, *School Library Journal* Best Book of the Year, and a Lewis Carroll Shelf Award Winner. His first three retellings of the Uncle Remus stories—*The Tales of Uncle Remus: The Adventures of Brer Rabbit; More Tales of Uncle Remus: Further Adventures of Brer Rabbit, His Friends, Enemies, and Others*; and *Further Tales of Uncle Remus: The Misadventures of Brer Rabbit, Brer Fox, Brer Wolf, the Doodang, and Other Creatures*—were all ALA Notable Books. The first two were Coretta Scott King Honor Books, and *Booklist* Editors' Choices, and the third was a *Parenting Magazine* Reading Magic Award and a National Council of Social Studies Notable Children's Trade Book in the Field of Social Studies. He has just completed writing *The Last Tales of Uncle Remus*.

Mr. Lester was born in St. Louis and grew up in Kansas City, Kansas, and Nashville, Tennessee, where he received his Bachelor of Arts from Fisk University. He has been a radio talk-show host, a co-host of a television program, and recorded original and African-American songs. Julius Lester lives in Amherst, where he teaches at the University of Massachusetts.